WICKET SEASON

WICKET SEASON

Gabrielle Prendergast

James Lorimer & Company Ltd., Publishers
Toronto

James Lorimer & Company Ltd., Publishers, acknowledges the support of the Ontario Arts Council. We acknowledge the financial support of the Government of Canada through the Canada Book Fund for our publishing activities. We acknowledge the support of the Canada Council for the Arts, which last year invested $24.3 million in writing and publishing throughout Canada. We acknowledge the Government of Ontario through the Ontario Media Development Corporation's Ontario Book Initiative.

Cover Image: Shutterstock

Library and Archives Canada Cataloguing in Publication

Prendergast, Gabrielle
    Wicket season / Gabrielle Prendergast.

(Sports stories)
Issued also in electronic format.
ISBN 978-1-4594-0021-4 (bound).--ISBN 978-1-4594-0020-7 (pbk.)

    I. Title. II. Series: Sports stories (Toronto, Ont.)

PS8631.R448W52 2012   jC813'.6   C2011-907309-9

James Lorimer & Company Ltd.,   Distributed in the United States by:
Publishers   Orca Book Publishers
317 Adelaide Street West, Suite 1002   P.O. Box 468
Toronto, ON, Canada   Custer, WA USA
M5V 1P9   98240-0468
www.lorimer.ca

Printed and bound in Canada
Manufactured by Friesens Corporation in Altona, Manitoba, Canada in February 2012.
Job #72982

For Lucy

CONTENTS

PROLOGUE

"Harry? Harry, are you listening?"

Little Harrison Ambrose dragged his eyes away from the pile of sports equipment on the gym floor. The other five- and six-year-olds seemed to have less trouble paying attention and sitting still than he did, but that was nothing new. At six years old, he already knew a few things about himself. One of the things he knew was that he wasn't a great listener. But he thought the problem was that *other* children took far too long to understand things. After a minute or two, Harry usually felt that he completely got whatever was being talked about and was ready to move on to the next thing. So he tended to let his attention drift.

"Don't you want to know how to use those bats and balls you're staring at?" asked the smiling man. He was holding a flat bat and a red ball. Harry longed to try the bat. It reminded him of an old airplane propeller, and he loved old airplanes. And the ball was red, Harry's favourite colour.

"There are eleven players on each team," the man said. "Each player can get a turn at batting and two batters are up at once, one at each end of the pitch, this rectangle in the middle of the field. When one of them hits the ball—if they hit it far enough—they both run back and forth between the two sides. Each time they both reach one end safely, that counts as a run. In some games, teams can score over five hundred runs!"

The man pointed out two sets of three long sticks that were set up like little picket fences in the centre of the gym. "Those are called the stumps. On top of the stumps are little blocks of wood called the bails." He passed a bail around so the children could look at them. "Together the stumps and the bails make up 'the wicket.'"

I get it, Harry thought to himself as he looked at the wooden bail, which was the size of his thumb. *The other team has to catch the ball and use it to knock those bails off before the runners get back to their . . . what was the word for it?*

". . . back to their crease," the man was saying. "If they don't make it, then that runner is out, and the next batter gets a turn. The fielding team—that's the team that's not batting—has to get all eleven players on the batting team out before they can bat."

Harry grinned. He was sure he could make lots of runs. That was another thing he knew about himself: he was good at sports. He could ice skate, run fast, throw and catch balls, do a somersault, and climb a pole better than any of the other kids in his class.

"The batter can hit the ball anywhere in the circle. Forward, backward, anywhere," the man said. "If the ball rolls to the boundary, that's four runs. If it flies over the boundary before it bounces, that's six runs. It's great when you hit a six, but it doesn't happen very often."

Harry planned to hit many sixes. He knew he could do it.

"As long as you don't get out, you can keep batting and keep getting runs," the man said next. "The most runs ever scored by one player without getting out was four hundred! By Brian Lara, a West Indian player."

Harry knew he could beat that record. How hard could it be? He could count to one hundred already, and four hundred probably wasn't much higher than that. Also, the highest score was by a West Indian. Harry was West Indian too, or at least his parents were. He wasn't sure what that meant, but he suspected it meant he'd be good at batting.

"Who'd like to try hitting the ball?" the man asked.

Harry's little hand shot into the air. He jumped to his feet before the man even called him up. Harry took the bat as the man placed the red ball on top of an orange thing that looked like a witch's hat. The man explained that once they'd had some practice, instead of hitting the ball from the orange thing they would be batting at balls thrown, or bowled, by a player called the bowler. And something about the ball bouncing on the pitch before the batter hit it. But Harry wasn't listening—he just wanted to hit the ball. When the man nodded, Harry stepped forward and took a swing.

WHAP!

The ball went flying. Somehow Harry had managed to hit it over his own head and behind him to the left.

"Is that a foul ball?" he asked, feeling disappointed.

The man smiled. "Nope. No fouls in cricket. You hit that to a part of the field called backward short leg."

Harry stifled a laugh. "A backward short leg would be hard to walk on," he blurted out, making the whole class dissolve into giggles. Even the man laughed. Harry felt good. He'd hit the ball and made everyone laugh. This was the third thing he already knew about himself: he loved having everyone watching and listening to him.

When everyone had settled down, the man went on. "One of the most fun things about cricket is all the shouting that goes on." Harry loved shouting. He listened extra hard as the man continued. "If the batter thinks it's safe to run, he or she will shout 'Yes!' If a fielder thinks he or she will catch the ball, they'll shout 'Mine!' When the fielding team think a batter is out, they yell 'How is that?' but it usually comes out as 'Howzat!'"

Harry liked the sound of that.

1 THE END OF THE SEASON

Tweet from @harrythehero:
I think I'll hit a six today. Great day for cricket. Hope it doesn't snow! **#ilovecricket**

"*Howzat!*"

Harry did not move from his crease. The other team's wicket keeper standing behind him could shout all he wanted about having caught the ball. Harry knew he wasn't out. He looked down the pitch to the umpire, who was shaking his head, a stern expression on his face. Harry grinned, feeling smug. Even though at fourteen years old he was the youngest player on the field, and the only kid, he was confident about his batting. He hadn't nicked the ball; he'd barely swung at it. He wasn't out. His team, the Winnipeg Warriors, needed five runs to beat Regina in the last game of the season. They had six balls left to make five runs. With five more runs, he'd also have a half century—fifty runs—to finish the game and the season. Easy.

Harry adjusted his batting helmet and tugged at his gloves. It was getting cold, and he wanted to wind up this game as quickly as possible. He looked down the pitch again to his batting partner at the other end. Milton was bouncing on the spot, trying to stay warm. Milton, who was in his second year at Brandon University, complained endlessly about the cold in Manitoba. Harry's parents, like Milton, were from the Caribbean, but Harry had grown up in Manitoba. He was used to the weather.

"Love the cold, Dawg," Harry yelled down the pitch. He tapped the ground with his bat and concentrated. The Regina bowler was a spinner, trying to make each ball spin so it would bounce wild and be hard to hit, but he wasn't a very good one. Harry thought he'd put poor Milton out of his misery by hitting the ball over the boundary for six runs. Then the game would be won and they could go for the Mexican meal he'd been promised. He had been looking forward to it since afternoon tea.

The Regina bowler glared at him. Harry had faced this guy before. He was old—at least fifty—and bowled spin only because he was too out of shape to bowl fast. Harry watched as the bowler stepped forward, swung his bowling arm up and over, and released the ball with a grunt of effort. The ball bounced in a predictable arc and Harry prepared to swing hard, but at the last instant, the ball spun inwards. Harry was forced to adjust his swing to prevent the ball from hitting his leg and getting called out.

CRACK!

Harry managed a pretty good hit. The ball rolled quickly away towards the boundary. The small crowd of players and spectators yelled and applauded.

"Yes!" Harry cried, as he and Milton took off running. Harry reached the other end of the pitch, quickly tapped his bat inside Milton's crease, and turned to run the other way. He could see Milton wasn't so sure about taking the second run, but Harry wanted to stay on strike and keep batting. He needed to get back to his own crease. Milton had no choice but to follow his lead.

A fielder flung himself down to stop the ball rolling to the boundary for four runs. He leapt back to his feet and threw a surprisingly accurate throw to Harry's crease at the striker's end. The wicket keeper caught it expertly and wiped the bails off with a sweep of the ball just as Harry dove for the crease. There was another loud appeal from the Regina players.

"HOWZAT?!"

"Safe!" cried the umpire, shaking his head.

Harry rolled his eyes, and several of the Regina fielders chortled. The umpire was still training, since he had called games as a baseball umpire. He had forgotten the proper call was "Not out!"

Harry's team had made two runs. Now all they needed was three runs off five balls. Harry still wanted to finish the game with a six—a nice high drive over the boundary. Not all the local cricket fields allowed for sixes, since the boundaries were sometimes bushes or ravines or gym walls. But the Winnipeg Cricket Club had just put in a proper boundary. Harry tried to hit sixes whenever he played there. A six was the home run of cricket, after all.

The Regina players were having a discussion on the field. Their elderly bowler had pulled a muscle bowling that last ball and was limping away. Harry grinned to himself when he saw his replacement. He was a young South Asian bowler he'd faced before. He was a fast bowler—a good one. But it was much easier to hit a ball for six off a fast delivery, if you timed it right. Harry felt sure he could time it right.

Harry adjusted his stance. He was determined that this next shot would go for six. He glanced quickly at two fielders near the boundary. They both looked tired and cold. Harry planned to hit a high drive right between them. *They won't even see it*, Harry thought.

The new Regina bowler ran in fast. Harry could see that he knew this was the last chance for Regina to win the game and the tournament. There was a fierce expression on his face that nearly made Harry lose his concentration. Nearly.

The bowler released the ball, hurling it down onto

the pitch with incredible force. It bounced straight at Harry—straight at his head, in fact. Harry suddenly found his head thinking more of not being concussed than of hitting a six. But his cricket-crazy heart took over. He raised the bat and swung, hard and precise.

CRACK!

The ball flew up over the heads of the infielders, who leapt up in a vain attempt to stop it. Just as Harry had intended, the ball sailed right between the two fielders and bounced well outside the boundary.

"Six!" cried the umpire, raising both arms in the air.

The crowd erupted into cheers. Milton raced down the pitch and grabbed Harry, lifting him up easily. Harry's teammates poured out of the clubhouse and onto the field. Some of Harry's school friends who had come to watch the match began chanting from the stands.

"Harry! Harry! Harry!"

Harry was in his element. He tore off his helmet, raised his bat into the air, and hooted with triumph.

Fifty-three runs in this game. His season average was well over forty. He had just made the season-winning runs and hit a spectacular six. Harry sighed with pleasure. He was a star!

2 DISASTER RECOVERY

Text message from Milton:
Pass the salsa. BTW awesome six!

Harry ate two beef burritos, three tacos, and half a plate of nachos before his parents came to collect him at the restaurant. They'd watched the game, of course, and congratulated him at the end. But they knew he wanted to celebrate with his team, so they went to a nearby bistro while Harry and his teammates devoured Mexican food.

"You were supposed to call us when things started getting boozy," Harry's father said. Harry looked at the table. He'd been so intent on shovelling food into his mouth he hadn't noticed the empty beer bottles piling up in front of his teammates.

"I didn't have any!" Harry protested.

"Of course you didn't," Milton laughed, looking at Harry's slight frame. "You couldn't get served if you tried."

Harry threw a nacho at Milton's head. "Bye

everyone!" he called out as he got up.

There followed a chorus of farewells and many slaps on the back. Milton burped loudly, apologized to Harry's mother, and shook his father's hand before Harry was finally able to leave.

"Classy lot," his father commented as they walked out to the car. Harry and his mother giggled.

The car was parked four blocks away. As they walked, Harry pulled out his phone.

"I'm going to call Pop," Harry said.

"Ask him about Thanksgiving," his mother said.

Pop was Harry's grandfather—his father's father. He was as Jamaican as jerk chicken, his father would say. He still owned the barbershop in Toronto that he'd opened when the family first arrived in Canada. Harry's dad had been a gifted high school student then, with dreams of university and a great career. Pop's hard work had helped those dreams come true.

"Harry!" Pop said over the phone. "I was hoping you'd call. How was the game, my boy? Were you the big star again?"

As usual, it took a minute for Harry to get used to Pop's strong Jamaican accent. "We won!" Harry exclaimed.

"Of course you won," Pop said. "But HOW did you win?"

Harry proceeded to give Pop a play-by-play of almost the whole game—at least all the parts that involved Harry. "And I finished off with a six!" he added, just as they reached the car.

"A six? That's great, Harry," Pop said.

"Oh hey, I'm supposed to ask you about Thanksgiving. Mom wants to know if you're coming."

"I'd love to. But I thought I might come at Christmas too. What do you think?"

"Sounds great. I'll tell her." Harry climbed into the car. "I've got to go. Dad hates it when I talk on the phone in the car."

"Right. Tell him I said hello. Bye, Harry!"

"Bye, Pop!"

Harry tucked his phone away and buckled up. "Yes to Thanksgiving, but he wants to come for Christmas too," Harry said.

Harry parents looked at each other. "Oh, okay," his mother said.

Harry's father pulled the car out of the parking lot and they drove in silence for a few minutes.

"Well, it would be nice to see him again at Christmas, since ..." Harry's dad started.

"*Ben*," his mother whispered.

Harry hated it when his parents acted like this. Obviously there was something going on. If it was something about Pop, Harry wanted to know.

"Is Pop okay?" he asked.

"Of course he is, cher. He's fine," his mother said. "We have some news, that's all."

Harry's mind raced. Is someone sick? Maybe his

mother was having a baby! *A brother or sister? How awful*, Harry thought.

Harry's dad snapped him out of his horrifying daydream. "I've been offered a research grant to study disaster recovery."

"Oh," Harry said. "That's good, right? That's what you teach at Brandon U. So is it like a promotion or something?"

"It's a travel grant. For six months, starting in January."

"Six months! You're going to leave us for six months?! You can't. What about Mom?"

Harry's parents were silent for a moment. "I'm going too, cher. To do some nursing," his mom said, finally.

"Wait. I don't get it," Harry said, confused. "You're leaving me here alone? You can't do that. I'm only fourteen!"

"We're all going to go," Harry's mom said with a smile.

It sounded to Harry like his parents had made a big decision about his life without consulting him. Still, maybe a trip might not be so bad. Maybe they were going to England or Australia. He could play some awesome cricket there. "Where are we going?" he asked.

"Well, Haiti," his dad said.

Harry was speechless. His mom was Haitian, and even she hadn't been back there in years. Haiti was a mess. It had always been a mess, from what Harry had heard from his relatives. And although Harry spoke French with his mother sometimes, he wasn't very good at it. And they didn't play cricket in Haiti.

"No way!" Harry blurted out. "It's terrible there!"

"That's why we're going. To help them."

"YOU go then. What can I do to help them? They probably don't even have schools or anything! What about cricket? I'll miss half the season!"

"Maybe you could teach cricket to the orphans or something," Harry's father suggested. "They would love that."

"I'm not wasting my talent on little twerps."

"You were a little twerp once," his father pointed out. "Wouldn't you like to make a difference in their lives?"

"I'm NOT going!" Harry declared.

"Harry . . ." his mother said softly.

But Harry refused to speak to them for the rest of the ride home.

When they finally arrived, it was nearly midnight. Harry retreated to his room without saying another word. He could hear his parents talking in hushed tones downstairs as he chose some hip hop from the music on his laptop and turned it up loud. One of his parents was sure to tell him to turn it off and go to bed soon, but he didn't care. He flopped down on his bed and brooded.

When he turned off his light, he could see a trace of aurora borealis in the sky out his window—the northern lights. He'd always loved them. He loved the Prairies. He loved the cold winters and the hot summers and the space. He loved his cricket club and the way they valued him. He was one of their best players. He loved his school. He was pretty popular and the girls thought he was "exotic."

Despite what he'd said in the car, he did care about his mother's homeland, Haiti. And he was a little curious about living there. But even though Harry sometimes felt special because he was different, he was a Canadian kid. He really didn't want to leave his home. He didn't want to be apart from his parents, but he didn't want to leave his friends, either. He definitely didn't want to miss almost a whole season of cricket. He didn't know what to do.

3 GIVING THANKS

E-mail message from: kingstonbarber@yahoo.ca
Subject: Haiti

Dear Harry,

You have a lot to offer in Haiti too. I read about some high
school kids who took a trip there to teach reading and writing.
Why don't you think about it?

Life goes on outside your little world, you know. It wouldn't
hurt to get out and try something new. Call me to talk about it
sometime.

Love,
Pop

Harry barely spoke to his parents over the next
month. He could see they were proceeding with
their plans—checking out airlines and buying

supplies—despite his disapproval. He had no idea what they had in mind for him in Haiti. All he had managed to figure out was that they were planning on heading there just after Christmas. That's what his mom meant when she said it would be nice to see Pop again over the holidays.

Harry had spoken to Pop on the phone about the plan, and told him how unhappy he was.

"Your father's career is important to him," Pop had said. "This is what he's worked for. It's what I worked for too, all those years."

"But what about me?" Harry had asked. "What about what's important to me? My friends, and school, and cricket?"

"It's only six months, Harry. Cricket will still be there when you get back. So will school."

"But what if I fall behind? Or miss important lessons?" Harry had argued. "They don't have proper schools in Haiti."

"You'll just have to work a bit harder to catch up when you come back," Pop had said.

"Hard work is what I'm trying to *avoid*, Pop."

"All the more reason for you to go."

"You ARE on their side. No one cares what I want!" Harry had yelled, before hanging up angrily.

Harry really did feel like no one cared, or understood how he felt. His parents and Pop had probably forgotten what it was like to be fourteen—how hard it was to fit in and find something that mattered. Cricket mattered to him. It was what he was good at. But it was more than that. Cricket was what made Harry unlike other kids. Sure, he played baseball at school—he was even pretty good at it. But cricket gave him an air of mystery that he liked. And so few kids played cricket in Winnipeg that Harry got noticed for his talent all the time. That mattered to him.

Also, though he didn't want to admit it to himself, he was worried about going to Haiti. He'd heard all kinds of awful things about what Haiti was like—sickness, crime, people living on the streets. Why would anyone want to go there? He wanted to continue living as he did: comfortably, with lots of friends and an easy time at school. Breezing through French, dozing through English. Only math was challenging, and who cared about math anyway? Professional cricket players didn't need math.

Cricket was his life. It was all he ever wanted to do. He couldn't afford to take any time away from it. He was more certain about that than anything else in the world.

He just wished his parents would see things the same way.

★★★

Harry couldn't mope forever, though. Thanksgiving morning, while his parents were at church, his grandfather turned up in a rented car.

"Hi, Pop," Harry said, giving him a quick hug and taking his suitcase down to the guest room.

"Harry, my boy!" Pop said. "You speaking to me again?"

"Sorry about that, Pop. I've been so messed up about going to Haiti and missing cricket. But it's not your fault."

"Don't think on it," Pop said. "I think I have a solution for all of us. We can talk about it at dinner."

Harry wondered all afternoon what Pop's idea was, but Pop refused to tell him. He couldn't wait for dinner to start.

"Pop's got an idea for me," Harry said just as they sat down to their feast. "About what to do while you're in Haiti."

His mother didn't look up at him. She carefully smoothed her napkin onto her lap. "We're still hoping you'll come with us," she said, quietly.

"Come on, Mom," Harry said. "I can't go to Haiti with you. I get why you want to go. But I need to go to school—a proper school. I'm not a good enough student to just bail out for six months."

Harry's mother looked up at him. "You really understand why I need to go?" she asked.

Harry felt his chest tighten. He hated to think his mother was unsure of his feelings for her. He would miss her and his father, of course, but now that he'd had time to think about it, he felt fiercely proud of what they planned to do for the people of Haiti. "Of course I understand, Mom," he said. "They need you there. I have everything I need, but they have nothing. It's only fair."

His mother's eyes shone. Pop was grinning proudly too. But Harry's dad still looked uncertain.

"You're sure you don't want to come along?" his father asked. "I could help you keep up with school work. And you could volunteer, really make a difference."

"I don't think I'm ready to make that kind of difference, Dad. Sorry." Harry hoped he wouldn't have to be more blatant about being just plain scared.

Harry's dad looked like he was going to say something else, but his mom interrupted him, turning to Pop. "So what is your idea?" she asked, serving him some pork griot.

"Harry can come to Toronto and live with me. They have a top cricket team at Eglinton High. They were city champs last year. He could go there."

"High school cricket?" Harry said. "That would be awesome!" Harry's mind raced. He could finally be a real sports star at school, like the captain of the football team. He'd have one of those jackets and his name on a trophy, just like in the movies.

"Harry's not going to Eglinton High, that's for sure," Harry's father said, interrupting Harry's daydream. His heart sank. What on earth could his father have against the school? It sounded great.

"Oh Ben, it's not so bad," Harry's mother said.

"That school's all street gangs and halfwits. It's even worse than when I went there."

"What about private school then?" Harry's mom suggested. "I work with an intern who graduated from Aberdeen Prep. He played cricket at school."

"Aberdeen Prep is a school for snobs and rich brats," Pop said.

Harry sighed impatiently. Truth was, he didn't care *what* school he went to, as long as he could play cricket.

"If medical interns are coming from there, then it's my kind of school," Harry's dad said. "Is it a boarding school?"

"A boarding school?" Harry said. "Why would I have to go to a boarding school in Toronto when Pop lives right there?"

"It's not the best neighbourhood . . ."

"I raised you in that neighbourhood," Pop said sternly. "You and your sisters. You all went to Eglinton High. I don't see why that's not good enough for Harry too."

"You know why," Harry's father said. "You know very well why."

Harry had no idea what they were talking about, but it was obviously something serious. On the other hand, it was his life they were discussing and he had a right to know what was going on. "Am I going to Toronto or not?"

There was a moment of uncomfortable silence.

"I think it's a good idea," his mother said. "Why don't we see if Aberdeen will take him?"

"And I can live with Pop?"

Harry's father took his time answering. "All right, then," he said to his wife. "IF and only if we can get him into a decent school."

Harry grinned and dug into a pile of yams. For the first time in weeks, he felt properly hungry.

4 IT'S COMPLICATED

E-mail message from: admissions@aberdeenprep.ca
Subject: Uniform requirements and dress code

Dear Mr. Ambrose,

Please find the uniform details attached. If you plan to join an outdoor sports team, you will need the correct footwear, such as cleats. Team uniforms are provided. Outdoor spring sports are baseball, track, soccer, and cricket.

All the best,
Janice Phillips, School Secretary
Aberdeen College

Harry was at the community centre gym practicing his bowling a few days before Christmas. He was so surprised to see his father appear in the doorway, he flubbed his delivery. The ball veered off course and rolled to his father's feet. Harry's father scooped it up and tossed it back. Harry caught it one-handed.

"What are you doing here?" he asked.

"Your mother said you'd be here. I thought we could hang out."

Harry was dumbfounded. His father never had time to just "hang out."

"Uh, okay," Harry finally said. "Do you want to bat?"

Harry's father picked up a cricket bat and Harry switched to a soft rubber ball to bowl with. Since there were no nets in the gym, he didn't think it was wise for his father to bat a tennis ball around, much less a hard cricket ball.

"Is that ball from the Kanga set?" Harry's father asked, after sweeping Harry's first delivery across the gym. The ball bounced lazily off the wall and floor and rolled back towards Harry.

"It's the only Kanga ball I still have. I lost all the others." Harry had gotten the kiddy-sized cricket set for Christmas when he was six.

"Your mother phoned all over Canada to find that set. We ended up ordering one from Australia," Harry's dad said.

"I still have the stumps and bails somewhere, I think."

"You should take it out to Toronto with you," his father said. "You could maybe coach some of the younger kids at the school."

"I hate little kids, Dad." Harry bowled a nice spin ball that his father failed to hit. "That would have bowled you," he said confidently.

"We would have loved to have you start with a Kanga league when you were little. All you ever had was that one lesson. It was given by one of my graduate students . . . what was his name? You were so excited when you came home."

Harry collected the ball that his father tossed back to him. "What's this about, Dad?" he said.

"What's what about?"

"All this talk of me when I was little, Kanga cricket and all that."

Harry's father lifted his bat and rested it on his shoulder. "Nothing," he said. "It's just that we won't be seeing each other for a while. I suppose I'm feeling nostalgic or something."

Harry found himself squeezing the rubber ball like a worry ball, over and over. "It's only going to be six months," he said, not wanting to meet his father's eyes. He had an awful feeling that one of them was going to start crying.

"You know why we moved away from Toronto, right?" his dad asked.

Harry shrugged.

"Toronto is very different from here," his dad said. "I mean in obvious ways, of course. It's bigger, more crowded, busier. Things won't come as easy as they usually do to you, Harry. At school especially. You'll really have to try. And cricket might not be all you're hoping for."

"What do you mean? I'm going to be awesome." Harry wound up and bowled the ball hard against the gym wall, catching it as it bounced back.

"I just mean cricket will be more competitive there. There will be a lot more people playing, more young people. The standard is very high."

"You don't think I'm good enough?"

"Of course I do, son, but Toronto is different. You'll have to make sure ... I'm not really sure how to say this without sounding ... bigoted."

Harry squeezed the ball again. "I don't know what 'bigoted' means," he said, honestly.

His father looked surprised. "You don't?" he said. "Well, that's what I mean. I think a boy like you in Toronto would know what 'bigoted' meant. It's basically the same as racist."

"How can you be a racist? You're black."

"Black people can be racist too," Harry's dad said.

"Against whites, you mean?"

"No—well yes, they can. But that's not what I mean. There's a whole community of black people in Toronto, of Jamaicans," Harry's dad said. "But you might find that they are not like us. You might find some of the Jamaican kids in Toronto to be a little ... rough."

"Rough? Like, poor?"

His father nodded and shrugged.

"So you don't want me to hang out with them?"

"It might be better if you didn't."

"Dad, you're telling me you don't want me hanging out with poor black people in Toronto when you used to be a poor black person in Toronto? And you are going to help poor black people in Haiti? Isn't that a bit Hippocratic?"

"You mean hypocritical?"

Harry sighed with irritation. "Yeah, that."

His dad took his time answering. Finally he set the bat down on the gym floor and walked over to where Harry was standing, putting his hands on his shoulders. "When it comes to your own children," he said. "A little hypocrisy is hard to avoid." He sighed. "I think sometimes people think that because you're black you need to be like all the other blacks around. Even other blacks sometimes think that. I'm just worried that the kids in Pop's neighbourhood will pressure you to do what they do—like running with gangs or doing graffiti. Or even just slacking off at school. I know from experience that it's hard to be different and be accepted when you're young. Just . . . try to make friends at Aberdeen, that's all."

Harry shrugged off his father's hands. "I'm old enough to decide for myself who to hang out with," he said.

"I knew you'd say that," his father said, with another sigh.

★★★

Over the next few days, Harry thought a lot about what his father had said. When Pop arrived for Christmas, he was relieved he had someone to talk to about it.

"Why doesn't Dad like Toronto?" he asked him as they walked back from the corner store. It was just before supper and so warm for December that Harry wasn't even wearing a toque.

Pop was silent for a moment, his boots making crunching noises in the moist snow. "That's complicated," he said.

"What do you mean?"

Pop spoke slowly, so his accent was easier for Harry to understand. "Sometimes your dad likes to pretend he's from a different family, from a different life. It's not his fault," he added quickly. "All that schooling has raised his sights. When he comes to see me, he stays in a fancy hotel downtown rather than stay at the old house. You've come with him. Didn't you think that was odd?"

Harry was starting to get angry at his father. "Does he think he's too good for you now?"

"He just . . . it's hard to explain. He wants to be a different person. He doesn't want to be an immigrant, a poor urban black man. Things were harder when he was in high school. There was a lot of racism. The police bothered him, even though he never put a toe wrong. In those days, people like us—black immigrants—we were the bottom of the pile. He wants to forget that part of himself. He worked hard to break away from it.

Now he doesn't want it for you. That's a big part of the reason he took the job in Brandon. To get as far away as possible. So the idea of you living in the old neighbourhood doesn't sit well with him."

Harry had no idea his father had all these experiences and bad memories. He only ever knew him as an important man, a respected professor.

They walked in silence for a bit. Harry was still troubled by something else his father had said, but he wasn't sure how to bring it up.

"Is Dad a racist?" he finally blurted out.

"What?! No!" Pop said. "Why would you think that? He has dozens of white friends."

"Not against whites. Against blacks. Like us."

Pop nodded. "Ahh, I understand. No, I don't think so. He's not a racist. But he saw a lot of kids go wrong in our neighbourhood. He still sees some of his high school classmates when he visits Toronto. They have kids your age now, and some of those kids have made bad choices too. He's just worried about you, that's all. He knows how easy it is to make friends with someone just because they look like you. He doesn't want you to fall in with the wrong kids. But I don't think he thinks *all* black kids are the wrong kids."

"How will I know who are the right kids?"

Pop laughed. "Leave that to me," he said. "I know everything and everyone in the neighbourhood. I won't let you get into trouble."

5 THE BIG CITY

"Mom, I'm standing right here," Harry said, reading the text on his phone. His mother just took his hand and squeezed it.

Maybe New Year's Day wasn't the best day to travel, Harry thought as they waited in the check-in line at the Winnipeg airport. Some of the staff looked bleary-eyed, and Harry's parents, who had been to a combined New Year's Eve and going-away party, were yawning a lot. But the line wasn't long, and they were all soon checked in.

It was time for Harry and his parents to go their separate ways. Harry and Pop were flying domestic, but his parents would have to go through customs.

"I'm going to visit the men's room," Pop announced.

"You lot say your goodbyes. Goodbye, son," he said as he and Harry's dad shook hands. Then he hugged Harry's mom and wandered towards the bathrooms. "Wait there for me, my boy," he called back to Harry.

Harry looked at his parents. The longest he had ever been away from them was when he had spent a week at YMCA camp. This time it would be six months. Harry wasn't exactly sure he could hold himself together as he said goodbye. He couldn't think of anything more embarrassing than crying in the airport in front of his parents, so he bit his lip and clenched his fists in his pockets.

Harry's mother hugged him, speaking softly to him in French. He struggled to follow what she said to him, but the general idea was clear. "I love you too, Maman," Harry said back to her, in French. He turned to his father. "I hope your research goes well," he said. "I hope it makes a big difference. You know, makes things better there."

His father looked into Harry's face and paused for a few seconds. "I hope cricket goes well," he finally said. They hugged awkwardly and Harry suddenly thought of all the times he had watched cricket matches while sitting on his dad's lap as a little boy. He had to bite his lip again.

Harry's parents showed their documents to the guard at the entrance to the international departures area. Then, turning once more to blow a kiss and wave, they disappeared behind the frosted glass wall.

Harry waited for Pop, feeling a bit miserable. The reality of living without his parents for six months had just hit him. He loved Pop and everything, but still . . .

"Something in your eye, my boy?" Pop asked, coming up behind him.

Harry hastily wiped his eyes. Pop put his arm around him encouragingly, and they headed down to the domestic gates.

★★★

It was already dark when they landed in Toronto.

"What time is it?" Harry asked as they waited for their luggage to come through.

"It's almost five," Pop said. "Do you want to stop and get some supper?"

Harry felt weird. He was hungry and not, tired and not. Part of him wanted to go out and explore the city and another part wanted to hide for a day or two, while he got his bearings. "Can we just go straight to your house?"

"Sure we can. I think I have some patties in the freezer I can cook up," Pop said.

They collected their bags and hopped into a taxi. Pop immediately started talking in Jamaican patois to the driver. Harry looked out the window, marvelling at the miles and miles of high-rise apartments they seemed to be passing.

"Ah, look," said Pop, "there's the CN Tower. See it, Harry?"

Harry turned. He could see something lit up on the horizon. It looked like a rocket ship to him. The city itself looked enormous and seemed to go on forever. Finally, they left the highway and pulled onto a busy city street.

"This is Eglinton West, the main street in my neighbourhood."

Harry peered out at the street. Although it was nighttime, the street was brightly lit and crowded. Harry marvelled silently at the many black faces, laughing and chatting with each other, going in and out of stores and restaurants, toting shopping bags, or dragging dawdling children. Apart from family gatherings, he'd never seen so many people like him together at once.

The taxi turned onto a quiet street. As they left busy Eglinton Avenue, Pop pointed out a small shop on the corner with a sign that said *Kingston Barbershop*. "There's my little kingdom," he said.

The taxi continued on for two blocks, then pulled up beside a small single-storey house.

"Remember my house, Harry?" Pop asked.

Harry didn't remember it being so small. It looked no bigger than their garage in Brandon. Would he even have his own room? Harry hoped so. Pop snored like a coffee grinder.

Pop paid the taxi and they dragged the luggage into

the house. Pop showed Harry his room, a cozy one on the far side of the kitchen. "This was your dad's room," Pop said. "He needed to study, so he didn't have to share like your aunties."

Harry looked around the room. It was about half the size of his room back in Brandon, with a single bed instead of his comfy queen bed. There was a little desk, a tiny dresser, and a small door to what Harry assumed was a closet.

"You remember where the bathroom is?" Pop asked, as Harry set down his suitcase.

"Yeah. There's only one, right?"

"There are only two of us," Pop said, with a smile. "How many do we need?"

After Harry unpacked his suitcase, they had a dinner of Jamaican beef patties with mandarin oranges for dessert. "I'll have to get some groceries," Pop said. "I'm not really set up to cook for two."

Harry looked up on the mantle at a picture of his grandmother. Pop's wife had died when Harry was a baby. He also saw photos of his father and his aunties, and of cousins and second cousins he had never met. Some of the photos were taken on the beaches of Jamaica and some in the snow of Toronto or the streets of London, England.

"Our family is all over, huh?" he said to Pop.

"It sure is," Pop answered. "Ever wonder where you'll end up?"

"Lords, I hope," said Harry, referring to the famous cricket ground in London. "Or maybe the SCG in Sydney."

"There's more to life than playing cricket," Pop said, teasingly.

"Not to me," said Harry.

6 COOL SHOES

E-mail from: c.ambrose@manitobahealth.ca
Subject: Haiti

Arrived late last night. Very hot. Very humble hotel. I have already started vaccinating people. Basically chasing hotel staff around with needles. Dad's still asleep. Will write more later and call tonight. Je t'aime.

Maman

Harry was awake when Pop knocked on his door early in the morning. "Come in," Harry said, sitting up.

"I'm going out to get some groceries. Want to come along?"

Harry showered and dressed quickly. Because it had snowed in the night, he put on his boots.

Eglinton Avenue was busy again. Pop looked in on the barbershop, which was closed for the holidays. He collected some mail and checked his voicemail. Then they headed down to the grocery store.

Harry tried to take it all in. Everything seemed so *old*. It looked like a movie set from the fifties—lots of quirky little stores and restaurants, with nail salons and coffee shops on every block. Harry half expected to see only other West Indians on the street, but this time there were people of all colours and ages. Dark-skinned women with braided hair pushed strollers with beaming babies. South Asian couples shared bowls of Vietnamese noodles behind restaurant windows. White teens hanging outside of cafés, busy texting on their cell phones. Asian men strolled out of barbershops with freshly-cut hair.

"Is this downtown?" Harry asked.

Pop laughed. "This is just a neighbourhood. Sometimes people call it 'Little Jamaica,' but as you can see, we have all cultures here now."

They headed down to the grocery store. "I might be a while, my boy," Pop said. "Why don't you explore and meet me back at home? You have your phone, don't you? And your house key?"

Harry nodded. "Are you sure?" he asked. He'd wandered around Brandon by himself for years, but this was different.

"You'll be fine. Anyone can tell you where the barbershop is if you get lost. 'Kingston Barbershop,' remember? You can find your way back from there." Pop grabbed a shopping cart and rolled it into the store.

Harry wasn't sure which way to go. He wasn't even sure which way he was facing. Uncertain, he started walking back the way they had come. Harry passed a few intriguing shops before he stopped outside a sports store, admiring a cool pair of green, yellow, and black sneakers on display in the window. After a minute, two boys approached him and spoke to him in very fast Jamaican patois. The traditional Jamaican greeting— "Wagwan, Daadie?"—was all he was able to catch.

"I'm sorry, I don't —"

"Oh, he Canadian baan, mon," said one of the boys, with a wide smile, switching to accented but more mainstream English. "You like those shoes? You Jamaican?"

"My father is," Harry said. He looked back at the shoes and realized they were the colours of the Jamaican flag. "Yeah, they're cool shoes." He turned back to the boys. "I'm Harry," he said.

"I'm Jordan," said one of the boys. "He's Oscar."

Harry bumped fists with both of them. "How old are you?" asked Oscar.

"Fourteen," Harry answered.

"Us too!" Jordan said. "You new? You going to Eglinton High?"

"I just moved in with my grandfather. I'm starting at Aberdeen next week," Harry said.

"Aberdeen Prep?" Jordan sang. "Who's your grand-father, mon? The king of Swaziland?"

"Uh, no. He's Desmond Ambrose, the —"

"Barber!" Jordan cried. "Kingston Barbershop! He's great. He styled me until I started to grow the dreads."

Harry looked at Jordan's short, spiky dreadlocks. He thought they made him look a bit like an alien, but decided not to comment.

"My mom cuts my hair. Number three clipper, once a month." Oscar said. "Why are you living with your grandfather?"

Jordan smacked him on the arm. "Dude, that's private," he said

"It's okay," Harry said. "My parents are working in Haiti for six months."

Oscar whistled, impressed. "They must be some good people to be going there right now," he said. Harry felt a rush of pride as Oscar went on. "Your dad a doctor or something?"

"He's a researcher. Mom's a nurse."

"My mom fixes school buses," Oscar said. "My dad's a runner. He ran away and never came back!"

Oscar and Jordan both snorted with laughter at this joke. Harry tried to laugh along with them, even though he didn't really think it was funny.

"My parents own the tailor shop on Dufferin. Wilson's. You know it?" Jordan asked.

"I don't know this neighbourhood at all," Harry said.

Jordan and Oscar grinned at each other. "Come with us, Harry," Jordan said. "We'll show you around."

They tramped through the snow, westward. Oscar and Jordan pointed out important sites along the way.

"Best patties here," Jordan said, outside a bakery. "Hot and spicy, but not too greasy."

"All the girls from Eglinton hang out here," Oscar said about a clothing store. Harry could see some young girls browsing the dresses and jeans, gossiping and giggling. He made a mental note to stay out of there. He didn't know much about girls, but he knew enough to never get in the way of their shopping.

"This is where the ladies get their hair done," Jordan said about a beauty salon. "My mother gets a 'touch up' every six weeks. I think she just likes it because she can sit around and gossip for three hours."

"Let's throw snowballs," Oscar suggested, as they approached Keelesdale Park. At the entrance to the park was a wide, flat field covered in snow. The boys quickly gathered snowballs and began pitching them into the trees, scattering sparrows and knocking snow off branches.

As they continued their fun, some older boys emerged from the trees on the other side of the field. "I bet I could hit one of them," Harry said.

Oscar suddenly became serious. "I wouldn't do that. They're gangbangers."

"Really?" Harry had never had anything to do with gangs before. He knew there was some gang activity in Winnipeg and some kids in Brandon dealing drugs, but he avoided them easily enough. He wondered why these guys, who didn't look any different from himself, had made such a bad choice. He was sure his father would have something to say about it. Surely these were the very kids he had warned him to avoid.

"They live around here?" Harry asked.

"Probably in the public housing," Jordan said. "Don't worry about them, though. Once they know you go to Aberdeen, they'll leave you alone. They don't go after no rich kids. That's a good way to get the police on you real fast."

"I'm not really rich," Harry said, embarrassed.

"Sure you're not, Aberdeen Prep," Oscar laughed, as the older boys left the park. "See if you can hit that tree."

Harry pelted a snowball accurately. It exploded against the tree trunk.

"You've got a good throw," Jordan said to Harry. "You play cricket?"

"Yeah, a bit. Do you?" Harry said with a smile.

"Do I play cricket?" Jordan laughed. "Mon, everybody plays cricket here."

Harry somehow knew this is what Jordan would say. Part of him had been hoping to hear it, in fact. But as he watched Oscar and Jordan hurling snowballs, he started to wonder: what would it be like to be just one more West Indian kid who loved cricket?

7 GIRLS AND CRICKET

E-mail from: b.ambrose@ubrandon.edu
Subject: Toronto

Hi Harry,

How are you doing? Pop tells me you've made some friends in the neighbourhood. I knew the Wilsons. Jordan's dad was in school with me when it was his parents running the tailor shop. It's nice to see a business stay in the family like that. They are good people.

Lots of heartbreak around here. But hope too. The Haitians are very strong and spiritual. It's inspiring.

Lots of love,
Dad

"Have you got your lunch?"

"Yes, Pop," Harry answered.

"And your Thermos? I made you some cocoa tea." Pop and Harry were rushing across a snowy parking lot to the Mississauga Field House. There was a large banner rippling in the cold wind over the door: *Cricket Clinic, February 8th.*

"I've got everything, Pop. I spent an hour packing last night. Shoes, shorts, bat, balls, helmet, spare shoes, gloves, pads, snacks, water bottle, phone, wallet, teddy bear, extra socks, chewing gum . . ."

"Wait. Teddy bear?" Pop asked.

"Just making sure you were listening," Harry said, with a grin.

They reached the doorway just as Jordan ambled up behind them, singing and swaying to some song he had playing on his mp3 player.

"WAGWAN, HARRY?" he shouted loudly, making Harry wince. Jordan removed his headphones. "Sorry, mon. Blessings, suh," Jordan said to Pop.

Pop said a few sentences in patois too fast for Harry to understand. Jordan answered just as fast, but this time Harry managed to discern that they were discussing Jordan's parents.

"Well, I'll leave you boys to your clinic now," Pop said. "Jordan do you want a ride home with us? Save your parents the trip?"

"That'd be great, suh!" Jordan said.

"I'll just go speak to your mother, then. Bye, Harry." Pop headed back down the stairs, waving at Jordan's mom, who was parked nearby.

"Oscar's not coming?" Harry said.

"No. His mom can't afford it." Jordan answered as they pushed through the doors into the Field House.

"Oh. That's too bad." Jordan shrugged off his winter coat, revealing a new hoodie beneath. "Hey, nice hoodie," Harry said. "Where'd you get it?"

Jordan modelled the hoodie proudly. It was black with a green and yellow X on the front that Harry recognized as based on the Jamaican flag. "My parents made it in the shop. They're going to sell them at Caribana this summer. You got to represent, right?"

"I guess so," Harry said. He wondered whether Jordan's parents could design a hoodie that was Jamaican *and* Canadian *and* Haitian. Just the thought of all the flags mixed together made Harry's eyes hurt.

Harry spotted some boys from Aberdeen Prep just inside the Field House.

"Who's that?" Jordan asked, as the older boys approached.

"Patrick somebody," Harry whispered. "Goes to Aberdeen. His dad's some kind of big sports promoter. Works with the Jays and the Argos and stuff. The other kid I don't know."

Patrick held out his hand when he reached them. "It's Harry, right? We have library at the same time. I'm Patrick." He indicated the dark-skinned boy with him. "This is Sanjay." Harry shook their hands politely.

"This is Jordan. He's goes to Eglinton."

"S'up?" Patrick said as he shook Jordan's hand. "I *thought* you might be into cricket," he said, turning back to Harry. "I mean, lots of . . ." he trailed off. "I mean . . ."

"Lots of blacks are into it?"

Patrick looked abashed. "That didn't come out right," he said.

"Nice racial profiling, Paddy," Sanjay said with a chuckle. Patrick blushed.

"Don't worry, mon," Jordan said. "It's true! You have excellent powers of observation."

"Yeah, thanks. Mention that to my mom, would you?" Patrick said with a sheepish smile. "Well, see you later," he said, before he and Sanjay returned to their friends.

Just then, a large group of girls arrived. Harry was surprised to see they were toting bats and helmets. Several were wearing cricket colours from India, Sri Lanka, and Pakistan.

"There's *girls* here," Harry said.

"I noticed," Jordan said. "This clinic is turning out even better than I thought."

As more kids trailed in, Harry grew more and more excited. Finally, when there were at least forty boys and about ten girls, the coaches came out. It took a few moments for them to settle the crowd down. When everyone was seated, one of the coaches, a tall South Asian man who introduced himself as Roshan, explained how the clinic was going to work.

"We're breaking into four groups. Each group will rotate through each workshop once. The workshops will focus on batting, fielding, bowling, and conditioning." Roshan proceeded to number everyone from one to four. Harry ended up being in group one with both Patrick and Sanjay, while Jordan was in group two.

"See you at lunch!" Jordan said, as he wandered off to the bowling workshop. Harry's group had the batting workshop first. They headed down to the end of the field, where some batting nets and an artificial pitch were set up. After they had warmed up with a junior coach, Roshan joined them.

"Okay, we're going to start with handling spinners. Who's got a good spin?"

A pretty Indian girl shot her hand up. Roshan called her up and introduced her. "This is Deepa from Scarborough High, everyone. Watch out for her." Deepa grinned and took the ball from him, stepping back to the bowler's end of the pitch.

"Anyone keen to face Deepa?" Roshan asked.

No one put their hand up. Several girls in the back giggled until Deepa glared at them. Behind him, Harry heard Patrick whisper, "I'm not up for humiliation today." Sanjay stifled a laugh. Harry wondered what they were talking about. He wasn't afraid to face Deepa. She was a *girl*, after all. He'd just hesitated out of politeness. Finally, he put his hand up.

"Ah, excellent. Harry, is it?" Roshan said. "Take your position please. Now, when facing a spinner, what are some things to remember?"

"Know what balls he can bowl," Harry said, confidently. He stood in the crease with his bat ready.

"Don't you mean what *she* can bowl?" Deepa said, tossing the ball from hand to hand.

"Yeah, sorry. *She*," Harry said.

"Good, okay," Roshan said. "What if you don't know what she can bowl?"

"Uh . . ." Harry wasn't sure. No one had ever asked him questions like this before. He'd never studied cricket like it was a subject in school. He'd just picked up a bat and started playing. Since he knew most of the players in Manitoba, he rarely faced someone whose bowling style he didn't know. "I don't know. Um . . . be prepared to move forward or backward in your crease? Or to the right or the left?"

"Yes, that might help. Let's try it. Deepa, if you please?"

Deepa stepped back a few paces and took a moment to size Harry up. Harry adjusted his stance so he could move around in the crease wherever the ball went. He felt confident he could hit anything she bowled. He just needed to keep his cool. The only time he'd ever faced a girl bowler was when his mom used to play with him in the yard—and she was terrible. He clenched his bat as Deepa skipped in, hopped, swung her arm over, and released the ball.

It seemed to happen in slow motion. Harry saw the ball leave Deepa's hand, but then he lost track of it. He spotted it again when it bounced on the pitch. Then he lost track of it again. Harry had a microsecond to remember his strategy of moving around in the crease, but he had no idea which way to move. Finally, he took a chance and leaned to the right. The ball neatly bounced off the pitch around his left leg and wiped out the middle stump with the precision of a missile. The bails flew back and scattered on the ground.

Group one clapped politely as Deepa took a bow. Harry was speechless.

"Okay, Harry," Roshan said. "Any idea where you went wrong there?"

Harry shook his head. "No," he said in a stunned voice. "No idea at all."

8 HUMILIATION

Text message from Jordan:
I'm starving. What did u bring 4 lunch?

The morning only got worse. Harry was bowled by four different spin bowlers before he finally managed to edge something, and that one was caught by the bowler. Most of the other players successfully improved their results, but Harry felt his batting just got shoddier. Mercifully, the first workshop only lasted an hour, then they had a five-minute break before moving onto the fielding workshop.

"Don't feel bad," Patrick said, as he waited with Harry to use the water fountain. "Deepa is the best bowler in the girls' league. She'll probably get recruited by the Ontario women's team."

Harry didn't feel any better.

At the fielding workshop, Harry bruised his elbow diving for a catch he didn't make, then twisted his ankle trying unsuccessfully to stop a fast ground ball from rolling to the boundary. Finally, a straight drive from Deepa hit him so hard in the ribs that he lay on the field gasping for breath for at least a minute. He was grateful when they broke for lunch.

"Awesome morning," Jordan said as they sat down in the bleachers with their lunches. Harry sipped his cocoa tea and tried to smile. His ribs were still throbbing painfully, and he had no appetite for his sandwich. "I did about a thousand push-ups in conditioning. How did it go for you?"

"Fine," Harry muttered as Deepa plopped down in the bleachers next to them.

"Sorry about the ribs," she said.

"Don't worry about it," Harry said. He introduced Deepa to Jordan.

"I heard you go to Aberdeen," Deepa said. "They have a brilliant gym, and a pretty good ground too. Their varsity players are all crap though."

"Harry'll soon sort them out," Jordan said.

Deepa looked doubtfully at Harry as she nibbled a cold samosa. "You look young to go for varsity. Are you in grade ten?"

"Nine," Harry said.

Deepa smiled awkwardly. "Oh. Well, you might get in, I suppose. This summer the Ontario women's team was sniffing around me, so I think I have varsity girls' pretty much in the bag. I might go for boys' instead though."

"Can you do that?" Jordan asked.

"Why not? I'm good enough."

Harry silently agreed, but also sincerely hoped Deepa would not end up on the boys' team at Scarborough High. He had no desire to face her spin bowl again.

After lunch, Harry returned to the field, less confident than he had been in the morning. He had been looking forward to working on his bowling, but remembering his pathetic performance in the batting workshop, he was worried he wouldn't bowl any good balls. After a brief warm-up, the coach broke them into pairs.

"Sanjay with Courtney, Roger with Indira . . ."

Harry sat there with his fingers crossed, thinking: *Not Deepa, not Deepa.* He was well aware she was a better bowler than him, but he couldn't bear the idea of being outshone by a girl in front of everyone.

"Harry with Patrick," said the coach. Harry let out a sigh of relief.

"Let's go," Patrick said.

They jogged to the far end of the field, where they found a bucket of tennis balls.

"So," Patrick said, "spinner or fast bowler?"

Harry shrugged. "Either. Both." *Neither*, he thought to himself.

"Okay. Let's see your fast ball. My brain still hurts from trying to hit Deepa's spins."

"You had trouble too?" Harry asked.

"Are you kidding? She massacred me about five times. Didn't you see?"

Harry started to feel a little better. He stepped back and ran in, launching one of the tennis balls as fast and hard as he could. It bounced nicely off the artificial wicket and sailed straight to Patrick's front pad. Patrick moved his bat slightly and blocked the ball. It rolled away, sluggishly.

"That was pretty fast," Patrick said. "But I might have taken one run from that. Gimme another."

Harry grabbed another ball from the bucket, ran in, swung his arm over, and released it with as much force as he could. To his horror, he realized he'd mistimed it, and the ball sailed towards Patrick, handing him the gift of what cricketers called a "juicy full toss." Patrick smashed it away effortlessly. It flew over the barrier and into the bleachers.

"They'll find that one tomorrow," Patrick said, looking smug.

Harry tried and failed to bowl Patrick four more times before they switched places.

"Don't look so glum," Patrick said. "I *am* three years older than you."

Harry seethed silently. After a few bowls, Harry got even madder when he suspected Patrick of bowling easy balls that Harry could hit.

When the coach came over to look at their bowling action and offer some pointers, Harry was further humiliated.

"Harry, you're bending your arm incorrectly on about a quarter of your deliveries. With your arm bent, you could be chucking the ball instead of bowling," the coach said. "Be careful of that. The umpires in this league are ruthless with chuckers."

"I'm not a chucker!" Harry protested to Patrick as the coach moved on to another pair of players. He had never been accused of the illegal throw before.

"He didn't say you were," Patrick said. "He's just trying to help. I think that's what we paid for, right?"

Harry remained in a foul mood through the conditioning clinic. His ankle hurt in the running drills and doing sit-ups made the bruise on his ribs throb. He was grateful when the day ended and he and Jordan were waiting outside for Pop to collect them.

"What a perfect day," Jordan said. "I can't wait until the season starts."

"Yeah?" Harry said. "I was awful today. There's no way I'll make varsity playing like this."

"Really? I thought you were the star player in Winnipeg."

"I was. But maybe that was just because all the other players sucked so bad."

Jordan pulled two juice boxes out of his backpack, handing one to Harry. "Have a drink, mon," he said, unwrapping his straw. "And don't worry. You can train next month at Eglinton Flats with the Keelesdale recreational league team. Get your game up before varsity tryouts. They start training in March. They're all so old and out of shape, they need the extra time."

"Thanks," Harry said, bitterly. "That sounds great."

He brooded about it all the way home in the car. Eventually, Jordan stopped talking about what a great time he'd had and slipped on his headphones. Harry could tell Pop was waiting to hear how his day had gone, but he didn't want to talk about it. He just gazed out the window at all the high-rise apartment buildings going by, thinking each one of them must contain at least one person who played better than the great cricketer from Brandon, Manitoba: Harry Ambrose.

9 LACK OF FOCUS

Oscar3.141: Heard the cricket clinic was great.
harrythehero: Not for me. I suck.
Oscar3.141: Bad day?
harrythehero: The worst. Came home and my dad called. He was all "I told you so." Real supportive.
Oscar3.141: I rented DeathCrash III. Wanna come over?
harrythehero: Sorry. Homework. HOMEWORK! Me! It's a world gone mad. C ya!

In the second week of March, Patrick stopped Harry in the hallway at Aberdeen to tell him about a cricket training and demonstration session after school. Harry showed up a few minutes late, having stopped to call Pop and tell him he wouldn't be home until supper.

"I said three o'clock," Patrick said, as Harry entered the gym.

"Sorry," Harry said. He hurried to join the group of boys jogging half-heartedly around the gym. As they ran, Harry realized he was the shortest boy there by at least six inches. He wondered if he was the only grade nine there.

After their warm-up, Patrick sat everyone down while he ran over the rules of cricket with some boys who were unfamiliar with the sport. Harry daydreamed as Patrick droned on. He imagined a large portrait of himself in the pages of the yearbook. He supposed there would probably be some kind of award ceremony where he would win "most promising athlete" or something like that. Hopefully his parents would be back from Haiti in time to come to the awards, then afterwards . . .

"Harry? HARRY?"

Harry blinked back to attention. "What? I mean, yes?"

"Any ideas?"

Harry stared blankly. Patrick was standing at the front holding up a cricket ball. "About what?" Harry asked, helplessly.

"About the question I asked you," Patrick said.

Harry had no choice but to own up. "I'm sorry. I wasn't paying attention," he said.

"You need to stay focused, Harry," Patrick said, frowning. "Lack of focus is how someone ends up getting bowled by a girl."

The other boys laughed at this, and Harry felt his face grow hot. "What was the question?" he asked, through gritted teeth.

"Why is a white ball sometimes used instead of a red one?"

"White balls are used in night games, because they're easier to see under the lights."

"And why might we sometimes practice with tennis balls, or Kanga cricket balls?"

"It's safer. Cricket balls are hard, and can injure you if you're not careful."

"That's right. They're less lethal." Patrick carelessly tossed the ball he was holding towards Harry. Harry barely caught it in time. He glared at Patrick.

"Nice catch," Patrick said.

They began some batting exercises. Two wickets were set up, with two batsmen facing Patrick and Sanjay. They would toss easy underhanders that the batsmen would have to step forward to block. Each batsman would face six deliveries, then the next one in line would step up. Harry had done this exercise before. If you did it for long enough, it was like doing lunges in the gym. Harry thought some of the boys would have sore legs the next day.

Harry waited his turn in line between two tall boys.

"What grade are you in?" one of them asked.

"Nine," Harry said.

The boy sniffed. "You're a little young for varsity, aren't you?"

"I'm good enough. I've been playing for years," Harry said.

"That may be, but Coach Barter never puts freshmen on the varsity team. He thinks varsity is a reward for being committed to the school for a couple of years."

"I'm only going to be here for this semester," Harry said. "I'm going back to Manitoba in the fall."

"Oh well," said the boy.

Harry's turn at bat arrived. Patrick threw him an easy underhand full toss. Harry lunged forward and flicked the ball up high over Patrick's head. It bounced and rolled away to the back of the gym. Sanjay, who was already retrieving his ball, scooped it up.

"Just block the shot, Harry," Patrick said. "Don't be tempted to hit it up like that. If there had been a man fielding there, you'd be out. Also, you're out of your crease."

Just then Harry felt something zip past his legs, and the stumps behind him clattered to the floor. He looked across the gym at Sanjay, who was casually tossing his own ball from hand to hand.

"Wicked throw, dude!" Patrick shouted. Sanjay grinned as he jogged back with the other ball. Harry silently tried to estimate how far Sanjay had thrown the ball. He had been completely on the other side of a full-size gym, nearly a hundred feet away. And he'd hit the stumps precisely, like it was nothing.

After the drills, the more experienced boys, including Harry, teamed up to play a short match outside in the field. Though the sun was shining, it was still cool, but Harry was used to that. He was looking forward to playing with some players his age for a change.

"The best way for the newbies to understand the game is to watch us play," Patrick said, after picking Harry to be on his team. "Wanna open the batting?"

"Wow, okay. Thanks," Harry said. They were going to play with a real ball, with real cricket rules, to show the new kids how things worked. Harry quickly padded up and pulled on a helmet. It felt good to be in full gear again. He felt more like himself—like he could do anything.

"Okay," Patrick said to the boys watching as the players took their positions. "This is what's called a 'limited overs match.' An over is six deliveries by the bowler—six balls. Limited overs matches have a set number of overs—usually between twenty and fifty. We're going to play ten overs a side. It will take about an hour."

Harry stepped in to bat. Patrick was his batting partner, while Sanjay was going to bowl the first few overs for the other team. The fielding team spread out into their positions with Sanjay adjusting them as needed.

"Anderson, come in! Dravid, closer to the boundary!" he yelled.

Harry stood clutching his bat eagerly. He couldn't wait to begin. Just as Sanjay finished adjusting the fielders, Harry noticed Coach Barter come out of the school. The gruff Australian man stood by the side of the oval, watching silently.

Now Harry was a bit nervous. With Coach Barter watching, it was even more important that he make a good impression. He glared down the pitch at Sanjay, who was running in to fast bowl. Time seemed to slow down. Harry glued his eyes to the ball as it left Sanjay's hand. It bounced on the hard artificial pitch and veered slightly to the side. Harry lunged forward on his left leg, then leaned back slightly on his right, getting his bat beneath the ball. His bat connected with the ball powerfully, lifting it up high out into the field.

"Catch it!" Sanjay yelled. Harry had a terrible moment of panic. He'd been so keen to hit the ball as hard as he could that he hadn't taken into account where it was going. Now he couldn't find the ball in the bright afternoon sky. Would the fielder catch it? Harry couldn't bear the idea of getting out like this, in front of Coach Barter and all these players.

"Run!" Patrick suddenly cried. Harry tore down the pitch, still not sure where the ball would come down. Reaching the other end, he smacked his bat on the dusty crease and turned back to run the other way.

"No!" Patrick yelled. Harry dove for the crease just as the ball sailed in from the field, and a player caught it behind him. But Harry was well inside the crease. The keeper didn't even bother knocking the bails off the stumps.

Harry was actually relieved that Patrick was now batting. It gave him a moment to get his heart to stop pounding in his chest. He heard Sanjay run in behind him, hurling the ball down the pitch. Patrick blocked it carefully and it rolled out to a fielder, off to the side of the wicket. There was no run in it. Harry stood his ground, poised to run for the next one.

Behind him, Sanjay ran in again. Harry watched from the corner of his eye as Sanjay leapt up, winding his arm over his head, grunting with effort as the ball left his hand. It shot down onto the pitch and bounced unexpectedly to the side. Patrick lunged over and swiped at the ball, cracking it hard enough for it to bounce across the ground at knee level, right between two fielders.

"Yes!" Patrick shouted. Harry hurtled down the pitch, keeping one eye on the ball that was still rolling towards the boundary. Was it going to go for four? Harry reached Patrick's end, tapped his bat, and turned back, glimpsing Patrick barrelling towards him. They passed each other in a blur. Harry focused purely on getting back to his crease, before —

"HOWZAT!?" the opposing team suddenly cried in unison. A senior boy who was acting as umpire raised his finger, and the players roared in, falling on Sanjay with congratulatory slaps and high-fives.

Harry was out. He was confused for a second, not really sure what had happened. While he was running, he hadn't been processing what was going on around him, but now that he was miserably toting his bat back to the bleachers he was able to put it together. The fielder had stopped the ball before it hit the boundary and flung it back to Sanjay. Since Patrick was already safely inside his crease, Sanjay had lobbed the ball to the stumps at Harry's end, taking them out milliseconds before Harry reached the safety of his crease. In short, he was run out after one run.

Not exactly the impressive result he'd been aiming for.

10 COCOA OR CHAI TEA?

E-mail from: williamc@ontariocricket.org
Subject: Re: Keelesdale team

Hi Harry,

Spoke with the committee and because you're a minor, we can waive your registration fees. We're happy to have you on the team. Jah knows, we need all the help we can get. First game is at the Flats this Sunday, 11 AM. See you then.

— William

"We're putting you halfway down the batting order," William told Harry as the team huddled around a portable gas heater at Eglinton Flats, sipping hot coffee. William was the Keelesdale captain, a Jamaican man Harry guessed was even older than his dad. "We'll see how we go in the bowling. We've got a couple of decent spin bowlers. Can you bowl fast?"

"Well enough, I think," said Harry. He thought William looked a bit worried.

The two captains tossed a coin, and the team from Scarborough won. They chose to field first, so Harry's team was up to bat. Harry was a bit disappointed. It was cold, and he had been hoping he could get out onto the field where he could move around to keep warm. But instead, he had to huddle around the heater with his new teammates as the first two batsmen went in.

Harry scoped out the opposing team as they spread around the field. Many of them looked young and athletic. Harry's eyes fell upon the opening bowler, who seemed smaller and slighter than his teammates. Then Harry noticed the long black braid trailing out of the bowler's cap.

"Is that a girl?" Harry asked his teammate, Albert.

"That's Deepa Singh. She's one of the best bowlers in the province."

Harry borrowed a pair of binoculars and gazed through them. Sure enough, it was Deepa, from the cricket clinic.

Harry was not looking forward to facing her spin balls again.

The game started out well for Keelesdale. William opened the batting with a respectable thirty-one runs before being caught by the wicket keeper behind him. His partner, an Aussie student named Ryan, made nineteen runs, but was run out when one of the Scarborough players made a scarily accurate throw-in. Then Albert jogged in, and had to jog right back out again after being bowled by Deepa without getting any runs. He was "out for a duck."

"Bad luck, mon," Harry said as Albert tore off his pads, shoving them into his kit bag in disgust.

Harry padded up. If one more batter got out, he'd be going into bat. His pads secure, he jumped up and down on the spot. The day was starting to warm up, but Harry was still grateful to be able to pull on the thick gloves. He picked up a bat and swung it, loosening up his shoulders and stretching his back.

"HOWZAT?!"

Harry spun his eyes to the umpire, who raised his finger. One of Harry's teammates had just been caught out. Harry's turn to bat had finally come.

He jogged out to the pitch and took his position at the crease. Deepa was bowling, Harry noted with a touch of dread. He'd been watching her bowling all morning and he thought he just might have it worked out. Keelesdale were four out for sixty-eight runs, which wasn't a terrible score for league cricket. But Harry had a feeling that the Scarborough team was capable of much more. He would need to rack up as many runs as he could to give Keelesdale a chance.

Deepa walked back, turned, and began her run in. She was running pretty hard, so Harry thought she might be trying a faster ball. That wasn't her usual style, but Harry was pleased. Maybe he could hit a six off her first delivery. That would be impressive.

Deepa swung her arm over and released the ball with what seemed like a lot of force. Just as Harry prepared to whack a fast ball, he realized Deepa had tried to trick him. It wasn't a fast delivery at all—it was a slow ball. Deepa was counting on Harry mistiming it. But Harry adjusted his attack in a microsecond and stepped forward to loft the ball, whacking it solidly.

CRACK!

Harry felt a brief moment of panic when he realized he hadn't quite gotten enough bat on the ball to get it over the boundary. A fielder ran in to make the catch. Harry ran for his life down the pitch, keeping one eye on the ball. He exhaled in relief to see it bounce just in front of the fielder, who scooped it up and sent it sailing back to Deepa. Harry and his partner, a Jamaican musician named Ron, managed to take one run.

Now Ron was batting, bouncing on the spot to keep warm. Deepa bowled him one of her nasty spin balls. He swung at it and missed, but the wicket keeper didn't catch it and it rolled away. Harry and Ron had time to take one run, switching places so Harry was back on strike.

Deepa ran in again, this time with a Yorker—a ball that landed so close to Harry that he barely stopped it from smacking his toes. The ball rolled right back to Deepa, who picked it up and brushed it against the front of her thigh to polish it. She took her time moving back for her next delivery. Harry tapped his bat a couple of times and glared down the pitch, bracing himself. He could sense that Deepa had something up her sleeve. She kept walking back, and back, until she was much too far to run in for a spin ball. *She must be planning a fast ball*, Harry thought to himself. Then he wondered if she was going to try to trick him with a slower ball again.

Either way I'm going to hit this one for six, Harry vowed silently.

Deepa turned and ran in, her long legs striding lightly across the shorn grey grass. She leapt impossibly high, twirled her arm over, and launched the ball down to the pitch where it bounced fiercely. Harry just had time to think, *Nope, definitely not a slow ball*, before he swung his bat under it, lofting it high and far over the boundary.

"Yeah!" Ron shouted from the other end of the pitch. The ball landed outside the boundary, and Harry's other teammates hooted their appreciation as well. Harry had scored a six off his third ball of the season. He tipped his hat to Ron and his team in thanks for the support. Then he looked over at Deepa. Normally, a bowler who had just been hit for six would be frowning with frustration, but she flashed Harry a big grin that made his insides go a bit soft.

This is why girls shouldn't play cricket, Harry thought.

But he couldn't help smiling back.

Harry and Ron scored seventeen more runs before they ran out of overs and their innings, or turn, at batting was over. They broke for lunch and drinks before Deepa's team took their turn at bat. Ron had brought several Thermoses of cocoa tea, which warmed Harry and his teammates nicely after they had eaten. Deepa's team, who were having their lunch nearby, were drinking chai tea. Deepa wandered over, a steaming cup in her hand.

"Are you having hot chocolate?" she said.

"Cocoa tea," Harry said. "It's like hot chocolate, only better. Want a cup?" He poured her some tea in a Styrofoam cup. She handed her chai tea to him.

They sipped in awkward silence for a few seconds. "That was a pretty nice six you hit," Deepa said, finally. "I won't bowl a fast ball to you again."

"Thanks," Harry said. He breathed in the spicy warmth from the chai and wondered what to say. "How long have you been playing cricket?" was what he came up with.

"Since I was six. My uncle ran a Kanga cricket program in Scarborough. Now I run one."

"You *run* the Kanga program?"

"Sure, it's awesome. The kids are adorable. Did you do Kanga cricket?"

Harry shook his head and swallowed a mouthful of hot tea. "They don't have Kanga in Winnipeg. But I had a Kanga set my parents ordered from Australia. My dad and granddad taught me. And a guy came to the school once when I was I kindergarten."

"Kanga programs are great," Deepa said. "Your coach at Aberdeen . . . uh . . . what's his name? Barker? Booker?"

"Barter," Harry said.

"Coach Barter, right. He's crazy about Kanga cricket. Always trying to start new programs and promote it. Thinks it will change the world. It's a bit sad, actually. So few Canadians care about cricket. And then there's all the other immigrants from China or Vietnam or South America. They all love soccer, but with cricket it's just us South Asians and West Indians."

"And a few Aussies," Harry added.

"Ah yes, the Aussies. They really add a sense of dignity to the whole cricket scene."

Harry and Deepa both burst out laughing at the idea of dignified Aussies. All the Aussies Harry had played with were great players, but most were young, single men on temporary work visas, and a little uncivilized.

Just then, one of Deepa's teammates called out to her in a language Harry didn't understand. Deepa turned and said something back. "That's my dad, also my captain. He loves bossing me around."

Harry laughed. "Your dad's your captain? That's cool. I hardly ever even play catch with my dad anymore. He's way too busy."

"Yeah it's okay, I guess," Deepa said, a little uncertainly. Her father suddenly barked something at her again, this time sounding angry. Deepa's face fell. "I have to go. Thanks for the cocoa." She headed back to her team. Harry wasn't sure, but he thought she might have been a little embarrassed. He wondered what her father had said.

11 PIPSQUEAKS

E-mail from: deepa256@hotmail.com
Subject: Cricket, what else?

Sorry about my dad at lunch. He doesn't like it when I talk to boys. He only lets me play cricket with boys because he DOES like to win.

It was fun beating you guys today. I wanted to throttle someone (you maybe) when you caught me when I was one run away from a half century, but I'm over it now. Caught on 49 . . . jeez. No, I'm over it! I swear! ;-)

See ya,
Deepa

After one especially gruelling cricket training session at school, Harry went back to look for a missing glove. He found Coach Barter inflating soccer balls in the gym.

"That yours?" Barter asked, pointing to a glove on the floor by the bleachers.

"Yeah, thanks," Harry said.

"You need to keep track of your equipment. Cricket gear is expensive here."

"Right. I know. I'll be more careful," he said, setting down his gym bag next to the bin of soccer balls. "Do you want help with that?" he asked.

Coach Barter grinned. "Sure. My hands are aching. Bloody arthritis." He handed the Harry the air hose and Harry starting filling the balls.

"Harry, isn't it?" Barter said.

"Yes sir," Harry said, grabbing another ball.

"Grade nine, right? You're a good player. I know you're not feeling confident, but you could make varsity next year if you work at it."

Harry's face fell. "I'm not going to be here next year," he said. "I'm only here for this semester while my parents work in Haiti."

"Oh? That's too bad. Well, any team would be lucky to have you."

"We don't have school teams in Manitoba. I play for the Keelesdale rec team, but I'd really love to play in a school competition."

Coach Barter shook his head. "I never select grade nines," he said. "It's not fair to the older boys. They've put in so much effort. Cricket is about commitment and service."

Harry filled another ball. "I am committed. I can

put in effort." And then, "I could help out with your Kanga program," he said impulsively.

Coach Barter studied Harry carefully. "Can you be at St. Andrews School gym on Saturday morning at eight?" he asked. "I can't promise anything, but I could really use a hand. Are you up for it?"

"Absolutely," Harry said.

"Great. See you then," Coach Barter said, disappearing through the doors and pulling the bin in behind him.

Harry sighed and hoisted his gym bag. *What have I gotten myself into?* he thought.

★★★

Coach Barter looked up from his clipboard as Harry ran into the St. Andrews gym, panting.

"Did you run from the subway? I like your attitude already," he said, pointing to a bench. "Grab a clipboard."

Harry picked up the clipboard from the bench. The piece of paper attached to it had a list of names, most of which seemed to be either Chinese or Middle Eastern. Harry looked at the list. He'd been playing cricket for years, but he'd never played with anyone called Xiang or Fatima. "Are these girls?"

"Girls and boys. You'll find them in the lobby. I'm going to take the seven to tens. I want you to handle the four to sixes. All right?"

Harry's mouth dropped open. "Four to six *years*? You mean, like, babies?"

"Yep. The Pipsqueaks. They're new immigrants, so some of them might not speak English every well. There are Kanga sets in the bag."

Harry followed Coach Barter out as he headed towards the lobby. "Why do new immigrants want to learn cricket?"

"Why not? The neighbourhood centre was looking for activities. I suggested cricket. No one else suggested anything, so cricket it is. Good luck!"

"But do they know about cricket? Or care?"

"Probably not, most of them. Though I think there's some kids from India in your group."

When they reached the lobby, Coach Barter started calling out names. A kid jumped up at each name. In a few minutes, about twenty kids were heading off, with Coach following them. Harry turned back to the families waiting in the lobby. Little faces looked up at him expectantly. He sighed heavily.

"Come here when I call your name. Xiang?" he called.

A few minutes later, he was standing in the smaller gym in front of a group of tiny children. Harry thought they looked impossibly small, and wondered if any of them would be able to lift a bat, much less hit the ball.

Harry started them off with a simple game: taking turns hitting the soft Kanga ball off the top of a traffic cone. At first, most of them failed to hit the ball at all, despite the fact that it was right in front of them. But eventually, Harry thought he saw some improvement. Encouraged, he had them try some bowling. The balls went backwards, straight up, straight down—anywhere but forward, and nowhere near where they were supposed to go. Then he took the children for a run around the gym, because he couldn't think of anything else to do. Finally, they took a break to have a snack.

Coach Barter came over to check on Harry's progress. "How's it going?" he asked.

"Great!" Harry lied.

After their snack, Harry decided to have them race in pairs between the wickets he'd set up, as if they were going for runs. The competitive nature of this game seemed to appeal to the kids. They screamed and put their whole selves into it. Some of the boys even had to be called out for checking.

It was chaotic and a bit of a shambles, but the kids loved it. By the time their parents arrived, they were worn out and demanding lunch in several different languages.

"See you next week, Mister Harry," the little girl called Fatima said as she left.

"Next week?" said Harry.

Coach Barter came up behind him. "Oh, sorry, I forgot to mention. It's every Saturday until summer. Is that okay?"

Harry was about to tell Coach Barter that he had

to play cricket with his rec team on Saturdays, but in truth, they mostly played Sunday games. And anyway, a few Saturdays would be worth it, if it led to being able to play varsity.

"It's fine, Coach. I'll be here," Harry said.

When Harry finally got back to the neighbourhood that afternoon, he found Pop sweeping up hair at the barbershop. A laptop computer was open on the counter, and Pop was watching a cricket match as he swept.

"Harry, my boy! How was your day?"

Harry gave Pop a quick summary. A large grin grew on Pop's face as Harry told him about the kids.

"Pipsqueaks, huh? Did you enjoy it?" he asked.

Harry sighed and plopped down in one of the barber chairs, turning it so he could see the screen. "I came to Toronto thinking I'd be playing a higher grade of cricket. But I don't think I could get any lower than teaching it to five year olds. Back home, everyone was always impressed with me, or interested at least. Like 'ooh cricket, what's that?' and stuff. I didn't even need to try very hard."

"So try harder," Pop said.

"I do. I am. Here, no one seems to care."

"I guess you're not so unusual here."

"No kidding," Harry said. "I'm just another Jamaican kid who plays a bit of cricket."

"Is that so bad?" Pop asked. "And anyway, I bet

those Pipsqueaks and their parents care."

Harry shrugged. "I guess I just always thought I'd be special or famous or something. I thought I'd do it through cricket. But now I don't know."

Pop sat down in the barber chair next to him. "I felt that way about cricket once too," he said. "And I got far with it."

"You played for Jamaica," Harry said.

"Yes, I did. In a match against Barbados. We lost by an innings. It was disastrous. Some of my teammates got selected to play for the West Indies team, but I didn't. I just wasn't as good as them. I started to think maybe it wasn't the way for me. I had to choose another way to fame and fortune."

"But you don't have fame and fortune."

"I don't have fame? Boy, what do you know? Have you met anyone in this neighbourhood who doesn't know me?"

Harry shook his head sheepishly. Pop was right. Everyone knew him.

"And fortune? Don't have a house? A barbershop? A son who's a professor, a daughter who's a nurse, and another daughter who owns a store? That's not fortune enough for you?"

"It is, Pop." Harry frowned at the laptop as the players left the field for lunch. "I miss being a star, though."

Pop and Harry watched the screen as a crowd of tiny Kanga players streamed onto the field in their matching yellow uniforms, waving their little bats and grinning at the cheering crowd. Harry could hear the pride in the Australian commentator's voice as he described the scene.

"These darling little kids are the youngest of the local Kanga cricket program. They're always a crowd favourite." Sure enough, the crowd let out a great cheer as one of the kids hit a ball far across the field. "This particular program is for underprivileged kids, supported by local businesses. Maybe a future Australian cricket captain is among them. What do you think, Tubby?"

The other commentator began to answer as the program broke to a commercial for a mobile phone network.

"There's more than one way to be a star," Pop said to Harry, getting up and continuing his sweeping. "You just need to find *your* way."

Harry went to the back room to get another broom, to help sweep. When he returned, Pop was sitting again, watching the Kanga players.

"They really are cute," Pop said.

Harry just rolled his eyes and started sweeping. He'd had enough cute for one day.

12 FAST AND PAINLESS

E-mail from: b.ambrose@ubrandon.edu
Re: Kanga ideas

I was thinking about what you said about the Pipsqueaks. Sometimes it's hard for kids from different cultures to mesh together in a group because they look and feel different. I remember being on a soccer team at the University of Toronto that was half Jamaican, half Chinese. It was a fiasco until we got our uniforms on. Then we were united.

Maybe you could get little t-shirts for your kids. Just an idea. Ask Jordan's parents. They might be able to get you a discount from one of their suppliers.

Love,
Dad

Saturdays with the Pipsqueaks and Sunday matches with the Keelesdale team became part of Harry's cricket routine. Soon, his schedule also included regular after-school tryouts with Coach Barter. Harry could see in these sessions that the older boys, like Patrick and Sanjay, were better than he was. It was going to be hard to reach the standards of the varsity team. He hoped all the work he was doing with the Pipsqueaks would pay off.

Playing cricket on the rec team was relaxing for Harry. There was no pressure and, although he wasn't the best player on the team, he felt valued. And the team was doing well—they'd won three matches, their only loss being the one against Deepa's team. Patrick still ribbed Harry about getting bowled by a girl every chance he got, but Harry didn't care. In fact, he and Deepa had been chatting online. They'd often chatted when Harry was supposed to be doing homework or going to sleep. Sometimes they discussed what they were doing with their Kanga kids.

We have to take a bathroom break every half hour, Harry complained one Saturday night, after a particularly difficult session with the Pipsqueaks.

I spend a third of my time breaking up fights between the boys. What is it with boys?

No idea, Harry wrote. *Maybe Kanga cricket should be a contact sport.*

LOL. Oops, I should go. I have a match tomorrow.

Me too. Who are you playing?

East Missisaga, Deepa wrote. *Missasauga …*

Missesa … oh whatever, you know what I mean. Who are you playing?

North York, Harry wrote.

Patrick plays for them—that dork from your school. The dork from North York.

Harry couldn't help but smile at Patrick being referred to as a dork, even though he didn't think it was entirely fair. Patrick was pretty cool. *Are they a good team?* he wrote.

Not as good as my team, but no one is. Bye!

Deepa signed off, leaving Harry grinning to himself.

The next morning, Harry had to suppress a chuckle as Patrick greeted him at the North York field.

"S'up, Harry?" he said.

"Hey, Patrick," Harry said. "Nice field." He noticed there was a permanent boundary. He planned on hitting a few sixes.

"Thanks. Did you know I played for North York?"

"Yeah, I heard." He noticed Patrick had large padded gloves in his kit, designed for catching fast-bowled balls behind the batter. "Are you wicket keeping?"

"That's right. Be careful of edging the ball."

"Oh, you know me," Harry boasted as he left to join his teammates. "When I hit the ball, I really hit it. No nicks. I'll be mostly hitting them over the boundary."

Patrick grinned. "Bring it," he said.

Harry started the game fielding close to the side of the wicket, after his captain won the coin toss and sent the North York team to bat. Two of the North York players were out after making thirty-six runs together, which brought Patrick up to bat.

"Watch your head, Harry," Patrick said, taking his position. Harry's fielding position was not as dangerous as some, but it was close enough to the batsman to make him cautious. Patrick was clearly trying to make Harry nervous. But Harry could give as good as he got.

"Hit them right at me, Paddy. We can make this fast and painless."

Harry's teammate Ron was bowling. He had a pretty good fast ball, so Harry had to be on his guard. If Patrick got some decent bat on a fast delivery, Harry *was* in danger of getting hit.

Patrick swung and missed Ron's first delivery. Albert, who was keeping, scooped it up and nudged it towards the bails, but Patrick was well inside the crease. Albert tossed the ball back to Ron. Ron stepped back and ran in again. This time his foot was over the line as he bowled, and the umpire called a "no ball"—the ball didn't count. He bowled another two balls, and Patrick flicked the second one hard enough to roll away past Harry, who dove in vain to stop it. Patrick and his partner took two runs.

"I hit that one right to you, Harry!" Patrick taunted from his crease. Harry just laughed.

William called Harry in to bowl. Ron tossed the ball in Harry's direction and moved out into the field. Taking position at the bowling end, Harry waved to two fielders to come in behind the wicket keeper. If Patrick was swinging and missing balls, there was a chance he would edge something and get caught behind by the wicket keeper. Harry thought carefully about what to bowl. Patrick knew Harry's bowling quite well from all the training and practice matches they'd done together at school. He would be expecting a fast ball, since Harry had brought the fielders in. Harry thought he might try Deepa's trick and bowl a slower ball instead.

He moved back from the pitch, turned, and ran in, swinging his arm over and releasing the ball. At the last moment, he reduced the force of his bowling arm and the ball sailed down the pitch much more slowly than his usual deliveries. Barely blinking, Patrick stepped forward and cranked his bat hard against the ball. It came flying back to Harry so fast he had to duck to avoid getting clocked in the head. A fielder ran back and caught the ball on the bounce. Patrick and his batting partner didn't run.

"I hit that one straight to you too, Harry," Patrick said.

This time Harry didn't smile.

Patrick hit Harry's next ball for four runs, then edged the third ball as Harry had intended, but the fielder dropped it. Harry cursed silently as he strode back for his run in. Patrick was still on strike and glaring down the pitch at Harry as he held his bat in front of him.

Harry skipped in and tried something with a little spin. Patrick took a swing at it, attempting to sweep it down behind him. Harry smiled to see that Patrick completely missed it, but the ball bounced over the stumps to be caught by the keeper.

"Nice bowling, Harry!"

Harry turned back to the bleachers to look for the source of the high voice that had called his name. There in the front seat were no less than four of his Pipsqueaks, with their parents, who had come to the game to cheer him on. Harry squinted in the sun. It was Xiang, the Chinese girl, with her father, and Fatima, whose mother was wearing a headscarf and long tunic over loose blue jeans. The two others were twins called Balraj and Sadikha, whose mother was wearing a brightly-coloured sari under her spring coat and a Blue Jays baseball hat on her head.

"Go, Harry, go!" the four children cried repeatedly, as their parents laughed.

Harry's spirits lifted. He realized that playing with Patrick had made him tense, the way he was playing school cricket, not relaxed the way weekend cricket usually made him feel. As the Pipsqueaks chanted from the bleachers, Harry ran in again, launching a fast ball hard onto the pitch. There must have been a stone or twig on the pitch because the ball bounced wildly, and higher than either Patrick or Harry expected. This time it was Patrick who had to duck. The keeper snatched the ball out of the air and tossed it back to Harry.

"Are you trying to kill me?" Patrick shouted.

"Maybe," Harry said with a cheeky grin. The cheering from the Pipsqueaks continued. Harry could tell Patrick was unnerved, both by Harry's noisy supporters and by his near miss with a fast ball. *This next delivery will get him out,* Harry thought. He ran in, swung his arm over, and hurled the ball as fast as he could. It bounced off the pitch with a loud *thunk* and veered slightly off to Patrick's side. Patrick turned and swung, connecting with the ball, which went bouncing off. Patrick and his partner tore past each other across the pitch. Harry ran in to the stumps just as Patrick tapped his bat. A fielder scooped up the ball and sent it sailing back to Harry. Harry didn't have even a microsecond to think. He could see, almost in slow motion, Patrick's batting partner bringing the tip of his bat down in the bowler's end crease. Barely looking where he was throwing, Harry lobbed the ball past Patrick, who was still running, to the stumps at Patrick's end. The ball hit square on the middle stump, sending the bails flying.

"HOWZAT?!" Harry's teammates cried. Patrick hadn't quite made it back to his crease. The umpire raised one finger, sending Patrick off the field, run out for seven runs.

Harry didn't notice Patrick's irritated expression as he made the long walk back to his teammates. He was too busy waving at his Pipsqueaks, who were still chanting his name.

"HARRY! HARRY! HARRY!"

13 CHARITY

Text message from Deepa:
Meet me outside Miss India on Gerrard at 2.

"Harry! Harry!"

Harry stood on his toes to see over the crowds of turbaned heads. Deepa was waving to him from in front of a sari store.

"Over here!"

"There she is," Harry said to Oscar and Jordan. "Come on."

The three of them pushed their way through the crowd. Harry was relieved to note they weren't the only ones at the street festival who were not South Asian. Many local families of all cultures had come out to share in the fun. They were on Gerrard Street East, where hundreds of people were celebrating after a parade Harry and his friends had just watched.

"What are we celebrating again?" Jordan asked.

"Khalsa Day," Oscar said. "It's a Sikh holy day."

"Hi, Harry!" Deepa said. "You made it."

"I wasn't sure we'd be able to find you." Harry thought Deepa looked beautiful. He'd never seen her in anything but cricket gear, but now she was wearing an embroidered orange tunic and shawl over loose pants and sparkly shoes. "I barely recognized you!"

Deepa twirled. "You like? Come on, let's get a samosa. They're free."

The four of them edged down the street past stalls handing out lassi, tea, and sweets.

"Everything is free?" Oscar said, accepting a cup of hot chai.

"It's part of our faith, to be charitable," Deepa said. "We demonstrate it during the festival especially."

As they walked, Harry let Oscar and Jordan get ahead of them. They were eager to try all the free food and didn't seem to notice as Harry and Deepa lingered behind.

"How is Kanga going?" Deepa asked.

"I've been wanting to talk to you about that," Harry said. "I think I'm running out of ideas."

"Really? Already?"

"Yeah. I don't think I'm very good with children." They walked in silence for a few moments. "How old were you when you came to Canada?"

"Me? I was nearly six. Why?"

"I was born here. Well, in Brandon actually. We don't have anything like this in Brandon." He looked around at the festival decorations and crowds. "I mean, there's a multicultural festival in Winnipeg. We always go to the Caribbean pavilion, but . . ." Harry trailed off. "It must be nice to be part of a big community like this." A smiling lady handed him what looked like a small, sugary donut. Harry took a nibble and discovered it was both sweet and spicy.

"Cricket is our community," Deepa said. "That's why your Kanga program is so great."

"The kids have started coming to my games," Harry said.

Deepa laughed. "Me too! I have these Vietnamese triplets. Triplets! Can you imagine the cuteness?"

Harry smiled as he thought of how cute Balraj and Sadikha were. And there were only two of them. Deepa stopped outside an Indian restaurant and waited as a young woman handed out warm samosas wrapped in orange paper napkins. Harry was quite pleased to realize Jordan and Oscar were nowhere to be seen.

"Does your Kanga program run through the summer?" Harry asked.

"We run it whenever we can find the money and the space," Deepa said. "Last year we had a fundraiser so we ran it all the way to September. But this year we couldn't raise as much. That's the way it goes. Most people outside our community don't care much about cricket." She looked sideways at Harry. "I heard you were just doing this Kanga thing to impress Coach Barter, to get on the varsity team."

"Where'd you hear that?" Harry asked. Even though it was essentially true, he didn't want Deepa to think his motives were that shallow. And anyway, he was starting to think that his efforts with the Pipsqueaks were to impress *her*, not the coach.

"Patrick told a guy from my school who plays for North York with him."

Harry frowned. He wasn't happy that people were gossiping about him, particularly if Patrick was one of them. "That's not the only reason," he said. "Maybe it was at first. But now I really enjoy it. The kids seem to love it, anyway." He crumpled his orange napkin and threw it into an overflowing garbage can. "I kind of feel sorry for them, you know? I mean . . . it was hard enough for me to move from Winnipeg to Toronto. I still feel pretty lost most of the time, and I'm fourteen. Imagine being that young and moving from halfway around the world."

"I don't have to imagine it," Deepa reminded him with a smile.

"Oh yeah, sorry. It makes me think of my dad though. I don't think he had a very good time when he first came to Canada. People were racist, apparently, and he felt left out of stuff."

"Did he play cricket?" Deepa asked.

"He did in Jamaica, but I don't think he ever had the chance here."

"Maybe that would have made him feel more included?"

Harry nodded thoughtfully. "I hate to think of those little kids feeling lost and left out of things. I really do think the Kanga program will help, but I'd like to do more."

"So do more."

"That's what I meant when I said I was running out of ideas."

"Harry, you live in one of the most cricket crazy neighbourhoods in Canada," Deepa said. "I'm sure someone can give you some ideas."

★★★

That night, when he wasn't thinking of how pretty Deepa had looked in her orange tunic, Harry pored over the Internet looking for ideas for the Pipsqueaks. He browsed cricket sites, community action sites, and education pages looking for fundraising ideas and advice on working with kids. He barely stopped to eat dinner with Pop, gobbling down his food while clicking away on his laptop. Pop frowned at him over his chicken and rice, finally confronting him at the mango ice cream.

"This isn't school work, is it?" he said.

"Huh? What?" said Harry, through a mouthful of ice cream. "No, it's something for the Pipsqueaks."

Pop continued to frown, stirring his ice cream idly. "You're spending a lot of time on this. Cricket, training, these kids?"

"Yeah. That was the idea, wasn't it?"

"It seems like a lot just to get onto the varsity team."

Now it was Harry who frowned. He'd kind of forgotten about the varsity team for the last few hours. Instead, he'd been concentrating on doing his best with the kids. Somehow, he'd started to think that helping others to play and enjoy cricket was more important that playing it himself! When did that happen? He shuddered and shook his head.

"That's the whole reason I came here, isn't it?" Harry said. "It will be a big waste of time if I don't make the team." Pop looked hurt and Harry quickly backpedalled. "No, I don't mean it like that. It's just that this was the project, right? There's no point in bothering if I don't go all-out."

Pop raised his eyebrows.

"What?" Harry said. "You look surprised."

"I wish your father was here to hear that," Pop said.

Harry began clearing the plates into the sink, imitating his father's educated Jamaican accent. "'Everything comes easily to you Harry. You never have to really try.' Wouldn't he love to see me now?"

Pop just looked at him.

"What?" Harry said.

"You do a very good impression of him," Pop said.

"Years of practice," Harry said, which made his grandfather laugh. Harry sat back down at his laptop. "I can teach kids the rules of cricket. And some of them might end up loving cricket like I do. But what's the point if they can't play it? Or even watch it most of the time? It's never on TV here. No one knows anything about it. Half the time there's not enough money to run the clubs, and there's no money for Kanga."

Pop didn't say anything. He just sat there, listening.

"What someone needs to do is get cricket into the newspaper somehow. Or on the TV news," Harry said.

"What for?" Pop asked.

"Well, why shouldn't Kanga cricket be like Little League baseball? With teams everywhere? If more people knew about it, more people would play. More parents would be looking for teams. Maybe we could get a big sponsor."

"So you want to raise the profile of cricket a bit?"

"That's what Coach Barter wants, I think."

"What do *you* want?"

Harry didn't answer for a moment. *I want to impress Deepa*, he thought to himself. *I want Coach Barter to put me on the varsity team. I want to help these little kids be part of something.*

"I want to make a difference," Harry finally said.

14 DOING BUSINESS

E-mail from: barter@aberdeencollege.ca
Re: Kanga program

Harry,

I like your idea of uniforms for the kids, but we just can't afford it. Some of these parents are refugees and haven't got jobs yet. I'd love to try some fundraising, but I wouldn't know where to start. Maybe Mrs. Harris at school might have some ideas. She's the alumni and donor liaison.

It's nice to see you getting so involved in this. See you Saturday.

Coach

"Patrick! Hey Patrick!" Harry ran down the hall after the older boy until a teacher coming out of the staff room scowled at him. Harry slowed to a fast walk, catching up with Patrick outside the cafeteria.

"Hey Harry," Patrick said. "What's up?"

"Listen," Harry said, as they lined up for food. "Would *you* like me to be on the cricket team?"

"It's not up to me —" Patrick started.

"I know, I know. But if you could choose, would you put me on the team?"

Patrick thought for a moment as the line moved forward a few paces. "Yeah, probably. You're small, and you look young, but you're as good as an older kid. It would put the other team off their guard maybe. Cricket's very psychological like that."

"Right." Harry reached into the shelves and grabbed an orange juice. "So if I asked you a favour, something that might help me make the team, would you consider it?"

"What's your plan?" Patrick asked.

They helped themselves to plates of meatballs and macaroni. "Your dad's a sports promoter, right?" Harry asked. "I heard he works with the Jays and stuff."

"You want tickets? How is that going to help you get on the team?"

Harry shook his head as they moved towards a table. "I don't want tickets. It's bigger than that."

They sat down together and started to eat.

"Coach Barter is kind of nuts about cricket, isn't he?" Harry said.

"Oh, you noticed?" Patrick said.

Harry grinned. "He wants to promote it around Toronto, right? Get more players and spectators, get more people interested in it?"

"I've talked to my dad about this before. But he doesn't know anything about cricket. And he's way too busy at this time of year, with the Jays season starting up."

"He won't really need to do anything," Harry said. "Does he have any time at all this weekend?"

"We were going to look for a new mountain bike downtown on Saturday morning."

"That's perfect," Harry said. "Can you bring him by the St. Andrews School gym anytime between nine and noon? Just for a few minutes?"

"What for?" Patrick said.

Harry didn't answer. He wasn't sure if he wanted Patrick to know about his ideas beforehand. He didn't want Patrick to start pointing out right away why it wouldn't work, or say that it was a dumb idea. But in the end, he thought he could trust Patrick to give him the help he needed. It was for the good of cricket, after all.

"Did you ever play Kanga cricket?" Harry finally asked.

★★★

Harry bolted out of school at the end of the day and ran down to the subway. By the time he got up to

Eglinton he was hot and sweaty, and taking the bus to his neighbourhood did not help. Squashed in the back among other private school kids, university students, and shift-workers, he dug out his cell phone and dialled Jordan's number.

"Wagwan, Harry?" Jordan said, answering quickly.

"Are you out of school yet?" Harry asked.

"Of course. I'm just having a patty with Oscar. Wanna meet up?"

"Can you meet me at your parents' store? I'll be there in about five minutes."

Jordan and Oscar were waiting on the sidewalk, both sipping vile-coloured bubble teas, when Harry got off the bus.

"Stylin' uniform," Jordan said as Harry approached.

Jordan was wearing his Jamaica hoodie again, over a polo shirt. "Back at ya," Harry said. "Wagwan, Oscar?"

Oscar looked glum. "I didn't make the Eglinton High cricket team."

Harry was surprised. Oscar was a pretty good player, almost as good as Jordan, who had texted Harry about making the team as soon as he found out. "Wow, that's too bad. You wanna play with the Keelesdale club with me? I'm sure they'd let you."

"I suppose. Did you make your school team?"

"They haven't done the selections yet," Harry said. "We've had three weeks of tryouts, so I think we hear next week."

"I hope you make it," Jordan said, slurping his tea. "I can't wait to bowl you out for a duck."

Harry faked a punch at Jordan, which Jordan blocked karate-style. They began an elaborate stage fight on the sidewalk.

"Hey! Man with a broken heart over here," Oscar said.

Jordan and Harry stopped scuffling. "Aw, want a hug?" Jordan asked.

"Ew, no!" laughed Oscar.

They went into Jordan's parents' store, Wilson Custom Tailors. "Hi, Mrs. Wilson," Harry said. Jordan's mother looked up from her computer. "Hello, boys!" She said something to Jordan in patois that Harry almost caught.

"It's bubble tea, Mom," Jordan said.

Mrs. Wilson made a face. "How you can drink that, I don't know," she said. "How are you, Oscar?"

"Don't ask," Oscar said.

Mrs. Wilson didn't seem surprised by his answer. "What about you, Harry? Going well at school?"

"Pretty good," Harry said. "But I do have a little problem I was hoping you could help me with. I need some uniforms for a team."

Mrs. Wilson raised her eyebrows. "Aberdeen does all their sports attire over at Athletic Textiles on Spadina, don't they?"

"It's not for an Aberdeen team," Harry said. He

explained about the Pipsqueaks and the plans he had for them. Mrs. Wilson listened patiently, a little smile growing on her face.

"I suppose you have no budget for this?" Mrs. Wilson said, crossing her arms.

"Oh, uh . . . well, I have some money."

Mrs. Wilson got out a pen and a pad of paper. She grabbed a calculator from a drawer beneath the counter. "You want track suits?"

"Yes," said Harry. "Tiny ones, though."

"In white? Cricket whites?"

Jordan started to giggle. "That would be so cute," he said. Oscar shot him a strange look. "What? It would!"

"You're such a girl," Oscar said.

"Am not!"

"Are too!"

Mrs. Wilson glared at them. "Boys, I'm trying to do some business here. Go watch TV or something." As Jordan and Oscar disappeared upstairs, Mrs. Wilson wrote some figures on the pad. "We could do them in white poly/cotton double-knit. That's not very expensive, and I have a bolt of it out back. What about design? What do you want on them? Any trim?"

"I hadn't thought of that," Harry said. "Does that cost extra?"

Mrs. Wilson thought for a moment. "Maybe I have something left over." She opened a cupboard behind the counter and began pulling out large spools of trim and elastic. "What about this?" She slapped a large spool of colourful trim on the counter. It seemed to be made up of dozen of little flags, from countries all over the world. "It's left over from a job we did for the Olympic bid."

"That's perfect!" Harry said. He loved the idea of the little kids being dressed up in flags from all their former countries. He even spotted the Jamaican, Canadian, and Haitian flags on the trim.

"Okay then, I won't charge you for that. When do you need them by?"

"Saturday," Harry replied.

Mrs. Wilson nearly dropped her pen. "Saturday? *This* Saturday?! Today is Monday!"

Harry cringed. "Is that possible?" he asked in a small voice.

Mrs. Wilson shouted something into the back room in patois. A man's voice shouted back. Finally Mrs. Wilson turned back to Harry.

"We can do them for forty dollars each, plus tax. I won't charge for the rush or for the trim."

Harry tried not to let his face fall. He had about two hundred dollars in his bank account from saving his allowance, but that wasn't enough "Maybe I could work for you. Sweep up? Or hand out flyers?" he suggested.

"We don't really need any sweeping," Mrs. Wilson said. "And I don't like the idea of flyers. It's a waste of paper." She thought for a moment. "I would like to get our business name out there a bit more, though."

"If this goes the way I'm hoping," Harry said. "You could have your name out there in a big way."

"I'm listening," said Mrs. Wilson.

15 NO CRYING IN CRICKET

Dr. B. Ambrose: Sorry, I can't seem to get the video and audio working on this end. Our connection might be too slow. That happens sometimes.

harrythehero: That's okay. Pop's fallen asleep in front of the TV again anyway. This way I won't disturb him.

Dr. B. Ambrose: How's school going?

harrythehero: Fine. I finally managed a B+ on a math test.

Dr. B. Ambrose: That's very good. All that effort will pay off, you know. Still keeping out of trouble?

harrythehero: I don't have time to get into trouble, Dad. Homework, cricket, Pipsqueaks. I'm swamped. My career as a supervillain will just have to wait.

That Saturday, Harry presented each Pipsqueak with their own custom-made uniform. Jordan's parents had done a fantastic job. The suits had little zip-up jackets trimmed with international flags and the pants had a flag-trim stripe down each leg. The back of the jackets read *Pipsqueaks Mini-Cricket, Sponsored by Wilson Custom*

Tailors. All the parents were delighted, and the kids were bustled into the change rooms to try on the suits.

Since it was halfway through the eight-week course, Harry had invited the parents to watch the practice. While Coach Barter took his group outside, Harry decided to try an impromptu match right there in the gym. He felt confident the Pipsqueaks had learned enough about cricket and had practiced enough to make it through a mini-match. He took a few moments to review the rules with the kids, then he broke them up into teams. One team lined up to bat, using the traffic cones—Harry wasn't going to try letting them bowl again—and the game started.

First up to bat was Fatima. She was so little she had to roll up the cuffs of her new track pants, but Harry knew she tried as hard as any of the kids. She stepped up to the traffic cone with a determined expression on her face, raised the bat with some effort, and swung as hard as she could.

Smack!

The ball went flying off. Fatima's mother and grandmother cheered from the bleachers. Two fielders chased after the ball as it rolled to the other side of the gym. After scuffling a bit, one of them, Xiang, finally scooped it up.

"Here! Here!" shouted Viktor, who was fielding near the stumps. Xiang flung the ball back, missing Viktor by a mile. Meanwhile, Harry had to remind

Fatima and her teammate to run between the wickets, which they did enthusiastically, as fast as their legs could carry them. By the time Viktor had retrieved the ball, they had clocked up three runs.

"Stop!" Harry shouted when Viktor finally got back to the stumps with the ball.

Now Fatima's teammate, Trang, was on strike. He took a swipe at the ball on the cone and it bounced off behind him.

"Is that a foul ball?" Trang said to Harry.

"Nope! No fouls in cricket! Run!" Harry shouted, laughing.

Fatima and Trang tore past each other as about five fielders chased the ball. As they took turns trying to throw it in, Harry noticed Patrick come into the gym with his father. They sat down just as the ball sailed back to a player by the batter's crease.

"Wipe off the bails!" someone shouted from the stand.

Harry glanced over to the stands and smiled to himself, seeing Sadhika's father coaching his ponytailed daughter. Sadhika smacked the stumps over just before Fatima reached her crease.

"Oops, Fatima, you're out," Harry said.

Fatima looked like she was going to cry. Harry patted her on the shoulder. "No crying in cricket, unless the ball hits you in the head. You did well, Fatima. Go watch with your mommy if you want." Fatima grinned and ran off. Christopher stepped up to bat. He picked the bat up by the wrong end.

"Other way, Chris," Harry called. He heard Patrick and his father chuckle from the stands.

Christopher switched the bat around and swung at the ball, missing, once, twice, three times. He stomped his foot in frustration.

"Go Kis-oh-per!" a toddler, who Harry guessed was Christopher's little sister, shouted from the stands. The rest of the crowd joined her, encouragingly. Christopher clenched his teeth in determination and swung hard.

Bang!

The whole traffic cone went over, ball and all, and flew about ten feet across the gym. The audience, which had grown to include the neighbourhood centre staff, cheered wildly as the ball rolled away.

Harry glowed with pride as Christopher and Trang ran between the wickets. The kids and their parents were having a blast, and he spotted Patrick's father pull out his phone and snap a few photos. Harry was surprised and delighted how well the kids were playing. The whole thing was turning out to be a huge success. It was better than he could have hoped.

They played for another half hour before the kids started getting restless. They had all had a turn at bat and at fielding and were tired and hungry. Harry sat them down with their snacks and put one of Coach Barter's older kids, who had come in to rest a twisted ankle, in charge. Then he went over to talk to Patrick and his father as they prepared to leave.

"That was sensational!" Patrick's father said, introducing himself as Alan. "I don't think I've ever seen anything so cute."

"Thanks," Harry said. "I was hoping you'd enjoy it."

"Patrick tells me you're looking for ways to raise the profile of cricket in Toronto. Get more kids interested."

"Well, that's what Coach Barter wants," Harry said. "I'm just helping out. But I'm sure he'd be thrilled if we could get some TV coverage or something."

Allen nodded thoughtfully. "You go back to your Pipsqueaks. Patrick and I will have a word with Coach Barter outside." As they left, Patrick gave Harry a thumbs-up.

Harry checked on his players. Most of them were eating their snack with a parent. The rest were crawling all over Coach Barter's player, who was tolerating them with good humour, despite her sore ankle. Harry took a moment to catch his breath and gather his thoughts. He had no idea what Alan was going to discuss with Coach Barter, but he hoped it would be something special. He caught himself hoping it would something good enough to get him onto the varsity team. But a second later, when Balraj and Viktor begged him to teach them to bowl, that thought vanished from his mind.

★★★

On Monday, when the varsity list was posted outside the gym, Harry avoided that end of the school for the whole morning. During Library he could see that Patrick was trying to get his attention, but he ducked into the science fiction aisle to escape him. Part of him didn't want to know. He'd had put so much effort towards getting on the team that he didn't know how he would react if he hadn't made it. Would everything with the Pipsqueaks and all the training at school and with the rec league have been for nothing?

Harry was still stressing over it at lunch. He was sitting with some boys from his computer class when Patrick came up behind him and slapped him hard on the back.

"Congrats, dude!" he said. "Well done."

Harry turned and saw Patrick and Sanjay grinning at him. His heart pounded in his chest, but he tried to conceal it, acting cool.

"Well done what?" Harry asked.

"First freshman on varsity cricket for years." Sanjay said. "Nice."

Harry's mouth hung open for a second as his classmates congratulated him.

"I made it?" he said. He couldn't believe it. He was going to play varsity cricket.

"Your name is on the list," Patrick said. "Go check it out."

Harry quickly excused himself, grabbing his backpack and running out of the lunch room. He slowed only when he reached the gym hallway, despite two teachers and the janitor telling him not to run in the halls. When he reached the gym door, he stared up at the list for a long time. It was true. His name was on the list, along with Patrick, Sanjay, and twenty other boys. Beside the list there was a gruelling schedule of training and games beginning the very next day. While he was silently calculating the hours he was going to be spending playing real competitive cricket, Coach Barter came up behind him.

"Congratulations, Harry."

Harry spun around. "Thank you so much," Harry said. "You won't regret it."

"I know I won't. You earned it, mate. And I don't just mean the work you did with the 'Squeaks either. You're a talented player, and you've got incredible commitment. That's pretty special for someone your age."

Harry felt his face get hot. He wasn't sure what to say. Even though people had been complimenting his cricket for years, it meant more coming from Coach Barter for some reason. Maybe it was because he was talking about Harry's commitment, not just his talent. This time, Harry had been up against a lot of other players who were just as talented and committed. Maybe that was why it felt like the first time he had accomplished something impressive not just to others, but to himself. He couldn't help grinning proudly. He couldn't wait to tell his parents, Pop, Jordan, and Oscar—and, of course, his Pipsqueaks.

16 A GREAT DAY FOR CRICKET

Text message from Mom:
Just landed. Met Pop. Waiting for bags. Tired, but we'll be there in time to come to the match! Dad's excited. See you soon.

"HOWZAT?!" Harry and his teammates yelled. The umpire raised a finger and Jordan and his batting partner trudged off the field, scowling. Harry's teammates rushed together in celebration. Eglinton High were all out for 115 runs. It wasn't a terrible result for their innings, but now that Aberdeen were going in to bat, Harry was confident they could make the runs and win the match.

Harry didn't feel even a little bit bad for bowling out his best friend, Jordan. Jordan had caught him out for a duck in their last game, and gone on to make forty-eight runs of Harry's bowling. So Harry figured they were even.

The teams took a fifteen-minute tea break. Normally, this was a time for players to discuss the last innings and strategize for the next, but Coach Barter quickly excused Harry.

Harry headed into the stands, hardly believing the good timing of his parents arriving the morning of his last varsity match. He was disappointed that it wasn't the final, but still pretty pleased with how his team had done. Both Aberdeen and Eglinton had been edged out in the semifinals by Deepa's team—Scarborough High—and Brampton Tech, who were going to play each other in the final the next day. Aberdeen and Eglinton were playing this match for third place, which wasn't so bad, Harry thought.

Harry looked up and saw his parents waving from the stands with Pop, Oscar, and about twenty Pipsqueaks and their parents seated all around them.

"Beautiful delivery on that last ball, son," Harry father said as Harry joined them.

"Yeah, wicked," said Oscar. "I'm going to get some lemonade. Do you want some, Harry's family?"

"That would be nice," Harry's mother said, passing Oscar some money. Oscar edged out of his seat and headed to the canteen truck. Harry noticed him say hello to Deepa, who was sitting near the canteen, as he passed her. He felt a pang of jealousy until Deepa turned to Harry and flashed him a mind-melting smile. Harry felt his brain turn to mush and had to shake himself to come back to a sensible frame of mind.

"Oscar won the math medal for grade nine this

year," Harry said, trying to suppress the silly smile on his face. "Wish my math grade was as good as his."

"There's more to life than math grades," Harry's father said.

Harry turned to his mother. "Who is this guy?" he asked, pointing at his dad.

His father laughed. "Six months in Haiti puts math grades into perspective," he said.

Oscar returned with their lemonades and they all sipped happily, enjoying the sunshine until the break was over. A couple more shy glances from Deepa made Harry feel like he could beat Brian Lara's record when he got up to bat. He felt like he could do anything.

Harry's father came down to sit with his team when they headed up to bat. Harry was halfway down the order again, at number five, so he had time to watch the game a bit with his family.

Patrick opened the batting, hitting a couple of impressive fours and quite a few doubles before getting caught. Sanjay joined his batting partner and hit a huge six, at which the crowd roared its approval. But then he hit the next ball straight to a fielder and had to walk off the field, cursing under his breath.

"Sorry, Sanj," Harry said.

"What a terrible way to finish the season," Sanjay said, shaking his head.

"That's the way cricket goes, I guess," Harry's father said as Harry began padding up. It was getting warm out and Harry thought a swim might be nice later.

"What hotel are you staying at?" he asked his dad.

"Hotel Pop's Place," Harry's father said. "He's letting us have his room and he'll sleep in the girls' old room. It has a comfy sofa in it now."

Harry was surprised. "Are you sure you'll be comfortable there?" he asked.

Harry's father laughed. "It will be so much better than the residence in Haiti. We'll feel like kings."

Harry was going to say something about remembering where you came from and who you are, something deep and brilliant, but he decided not to bother. He was sure his father had many things to say too, but that could wait for another time. Instead they just watched the game as Aberdeen racked up run after run.

The score was three men out, three wickets for ninety-four runs with just four overs remaining by the time Harry was up to bat. That meant Harry didn't have to worry so much about getting out, since there were six other batsmen lined up after him. But he did need to worry about there being only four overs left in the game. That was only twenty-four balls. They needed twenty-two runs. They could do it, if nothing went wrong. But Harry knew that things often went wrong in cricket.

As Harry strode out to the pitch, he felt a kind of golden feeling run through him. *This day couldn't be more perfect*, he thought to himself. The sun was shining;

the weather was warm and breezy. He was in full cricket gear, with a bat in his hand. All the most important people in his life were in the stands watching. What more could he want from life?

When he was a few paces from taking position, he relived the brief conversation he'd had with Deepa just before the game, while her father was looking the other way.

"If you hit a six today, I'll go out with you," she had whispered.

Harry tried not grin stupidly as he took his position at the crease. He knew Deepa's father would never allow her to date. He wasn't even sure *his* parents would let him, so he had no idea how he and Deepa were going to manage it. But that didn't matter. He took a deep breath. *I won't try a six off the first ball*, he said to himself. That would be grandstanding. *When the time is right*, Harry thought.

17 SPORTSMANSHIP

Harry had to get his mind back in the game. His partner, Angus, was on strike. Jordan was bowling. He was tossing the ball from hand to hand at the other end of the pitch. He nodded a polite greeting to Harry before stepping back to begin his run in.

Jordan started with a medium-pace ball—not fast, not slow. Angus blocked it easily and he and Harry took two runs—three for nincty six. Jordan ran in again, skipped up, and sent a thunderous bouncer down the pitch. Angus jerked out of the way, swinging, but his bat edged the ball and he was caught.

"HOWZAT?!" Jordan and his teammates cried.

Harry didn't even bother looking at the umpire. Angus was out for sure and was already slogging back to the bleachers, unbuckling his helmet as he went.

"Four down, six to go," Jordan murmured as he passed Harry at the bowler's end.

"Bring it," Harry said.

Jordan ran in again, this time with a fast ball at Angus's replacement, Samir. Samir leaned in to try to block it, but the ball smacked right into his front pad.

"HOWZAT?!"

Harry couldn't bear to look, but turning, he saw the umpire raise his finger. Samir was out because his leg had blocked the ball from hitting the stumps—leg before wicket. With Samir's wicket, Jordan was on his way to a hat trick — three wickets with three balls. He had taken two wickets in a row. If he took another wicket with this next ball, Jordan would win a trophy for the hat trick in the post-season awards ceremony.

Harry wasn't sure how to feel as Samir trudged back to the bleachers. In Winnipeg, Harry had never had to play against a friend on an opposing team. This season, he seemed to have a friend on every team he played. On the one hand, of course Harry wanted to win the game; on the other, it would be nice if Jordan got a trophy. But this was a dangerous situation. Harry had seen teams completely collapse when a bowler was on top like this. He took a deep breath. Nineteen runs to go. At least one six. *Focus*, he thought.

Jordan's teammates were shouting their encouragement as Jordan ran in. Harry could see he was going a little slower, possibly planning to try something with a little spin. Darshan, the new batsman, stood poised at strike, ready to take a swing at anything Jordan delivered. Harry cringed as Jordan released the ball. It was a Yorker, a ball that bounced right at the batsman's feet. Harry knew Darshan would have trouble blocking it. Darshan sliced his bat close to his front leg, but the ball swung to the side, edged his back pad, and took out the stumps. The bails fell to the ground as Jordan's team began to roar.

Jordan's team and the spectators went wild. Jordan's captain and teammates leapt on him, slapping him and congratulating him. Darshan even gave him a pat on the shoulder as he plodded back.

"Nice one," Darshan said.

Jordan caught Harry's eye, an ecstatic grin on his face. Harry tucked his bat under his arm and clapped his gloved hands together. A hat trick was a rare thing in cricket. No other player in the varsity league had achieved one this season. It was something both teams could celebrate, in the spirit of good sportsmanship. Harry felt bad for Darshan though.

As the celebration settled down, Harry glanced up at the scoreboard. It was now six for ninety-eight. There were just over three overs remaining—twenty balls to make eighteen runs. His new batting partner, a talented grade ten named Vikram, stopped and had a word with Harry on the way to the crease.

"Feeling it today, Harry?" he asked.

"Totally," Harry said.

"We should get you on strike, since you know this kid so well."

"You read my mind," Harry replied.

Vikram struggled to block Jordan's next two deliveries, finally tapping one past mid-wicket and taking two runs. That was the end of the over, bringing Harry onto strike. They had eighteen balls to make sixteen runs. Not impossible, but tricky.

Just go for it, Harry told himself. *Get the bat on the ball.* Jordan and his teammates were having a discussion at the bowling end, so Harry had a moment to think. He knew he and Vikram could make the runs with twos or threes. He wanted to hit a six, but he was in danger of being caught if it didn't quite make it. Harry looked at the nicely laid out boundary line around the field. Although he longed to hit one over it, it was too risky. He'd make the runs with twos and hope Deepa would go out with him anyway. It would not be quite as glorious for him, but it was winning for the team that mattered.

An Eglinton grade twelve bowled six fast balls in a row. Harry hit the first two for two runs each and smacked the sixth one for four. Now they were eight runs away from winning. Jordan came back in to bowl to Vikram. Vikram tried and failed to get any bat at all on the next three balls. They still needed eight runs, but had only nine balls to make them. Jordan bowled two more balls that earned them one run each. Now there were seven balls left to make six runs. Things were getting urgent.

While Jordan's team attended to a fielder with a twisted ankle, Vikram ran across the pitch toward Harry.

"Go for a six," he said.

"Really?" Harry said. "We can make it with twos."

"Can't chance it," Vikram said. "You need to end this now."

Harry stepped back to his crease. Jordan was going to bowl one more ball in this game. Harry was on strike. If he hit this ball for six, Aberdeen would win. If he didn't, who knows what would happen? He might get caught, or out some other way. Vikram or the next batter in the order would have to make the runs to win. Could they do it? Harry had a feeling he was their best hope. He would get the glory if he did it, and maybe get to go out with Deepa.

Harry turned and faced Jordan, who scowled back at him as he began his run in.

"Go for it, Harry!" cried a girl's voice from the bleachers.

Harry suppressed a grin. Deepa's support set his family and all the Pipsqueaks cheering too.

"Harry! Harry! Harry!"

Harry had a strange moment where he knew that it didn't matter whether he hit a six or got out. It didn't even matter if his team won or lost. He'd accomplished a lot in the past few months that mattered much more. New friendships, a new closer relationship with his Pop and his parents, maybe even a girlfriend of sorts. And of course, there were the Pipsqueaks. Cricket in Toronto was everything he'd hoped for and more.

Jordan ran in and fired the ball down on the hard pitch, bouncing it slightly to Harry's right side. Harry sprang forward, lifted his bat back, and swung it in a powerful arc, lofting the ball high over the pitch, high over the fielders, high into the sky, high into the bright golden afternoon sunlight.

EPILOGUE

"Strike three!"

Harry chewed his nails. The Blue Jays were up by four runs at the bottom of the seventh, the crowd was relaxed, and the open dome was letting cool air flow in. But it wasn't baseball that was making Harry nervous.

As the disappointed batter jogged to the dugout, Harry glanced down the walkway at the long row of tiny children behind him. In the dim light, he could see their excited eyes. Jordan, Oscar, Deepa, Patrick, and Sanjay were standing strategically among them, all uniformed, like Harry, in cricket whites trimmed with international flags. With help from his friends and Patrick's dad, there were nearly fifty Pipsqueaks now. All attired in miniature uniforms sponsored by various Toronto merchants, they made a very impressive sight.

Harry took a deep breath. The Red Sox were two out, so if the Jays pitcher struck out the next batter, the inning would be over. Then it would time for Harry and his Pipsqueaks to do their thing. He couldn't quite believe it.

Crack!

Harry peeked out the walkway door to catch a glimpse of the pop fly sailing higher and higher into the air. The player at centre field was going to catch it. He was right underneath it as the ball began to fall. *Third out and we're on*, Harry thought. *Catch it. Don't catch it.* He couldn't decide. He was ready and he wasn't.

The crowded roared in appreciation when the catch was made. Harry balled his hands into fists and turned to look at his crew. They were all grinning and bouncing, eager for the door to open, ready to run into the bright lights of the stadium. Harry grinned back at them. *This is it*, Harry thought. *This is how I make a difference. Ten minutes in front of a crowd of nearly 50,000. Maybe some time on national TV. People down in the States are watching this game. Tomorrow morning, everyone will be asking themselves how they can get their kids into cricket.*

Harry took a moment again to consider the irony. He had loved playing cricket in Manitoba because it made him unusual. Coming to Ontario had changed all that. He wasn't very unusual in Toronto, and after tonight, he thought he might not be very unusual in Manitoba. He sincerely hoped lots of parents were watching the game. He knew commercials would likely air over most of the demonstration, but maybe some parents would see enough to get them interested. Then they might start asking about Kanga cricket. Harry fully intended to start a program when he got back to

Brandon. Yep, cricket was not going to be unusual for much longer.

"Ladies and gentleman, for your seventh-inning stretch entertainment, Rogers Centre and the Blue Jays are pleased to present: Pipsqueak Cricket!"

Then Harry opened the door and let the Pipsqueaks pour out onto the field before him. After all, they were the stars. This was *their* chance to shine.

BE A
PRO! KNOW THE LINGO.

The following is a list of cricket terms used in the novel. To find out more about how to play cricket, or to find a club in your area, check out the Cricket Canada website: www.canadiancricket.org

ALL OUT: When an innings is ended due to ten of the eleven batsmen being dismissed.

APPEAL: The act of a bowler or fielder shouting at the umpire to ask if his last ball got the batsman out. Usually yelled as "Howzat!" ("How is that?")

BACKWARD SHORT LEG: A fielding position close behind the batsman on his or her leg side, i.e. on the left if the batsman is right-handed or vice versa.

BAILS: Two small pieces of wood that are placed on top of the stumps to form the wicket.

BATSMAN: The player currently batting.

BOUNDARY: The marked edge of the playing field. Balls that reach the boundary are worth four runs; balls that go past the boundary are worth six runs.

BOWLED: When a bowler's delivery puts down the wicket, the batsman is out, or "bowled."

BOWLER: The player on the fielding side who bowls to the batsman.

CAUGHT BEHIND: When the wicket keeper catches a ball that the batsman has nicked or hit, the batsman is out, or "caught behind."

CHUCKING: Occurs when the bowler does not throw with a straight arm. Balls thrown or "chucked" with a bent arm are called "no ball," giving the batting team one run and one extra ball to bat.

CREASE: The safe area behind a line at the end of the pitch for the batsmen. Also the area from which the bowler must bowl.

DELIVERY: One throw or bowled ball. There are six deliveries in an over.

DUCK: When a batsman is out before getting any runs, as in "he is out for a duck."

FIELDER: A player on the fielding side who is neither the wicket keeper nor the bowler.

FULL TOSS: A delivery that the batsman can hit before it bounces.

HALF CENTURY: A batsman's score of 50 runs in one innings. A score of 100 is called a century.

INNINGS: One player's or one team's turn to bat (or bowl). Unlike in baseball, in cricket the term "innings" is both singular and plural.

KANGA CRICKET: A simplified form of the game,

specifically designed to introduce children to the sport. It includes special equipment, like soft rubber balls, plastic wickets, and smaller bats. It can also be called Kwik Cricket or Kiwi Cricket.

LEG BEFORE WICKET (LBW): When the umpire determines that a ball would have taken out the stumps had the batter's leg or leg pad not been in the way, the batter is out due to leg before wicket.

LIMITED OVERS: A match where each side faces a set number of overs. A limited overs match is usually 10, 20, 30, 40, or 50 overs a side, and can be completed in a single day.

NO BALL: An illegal delivery, such as a chucked ball or when the bowler's foot is out of the bowling crease. The batting team is given one run and an extra ball to bat.

OVER: Consists of six balls delivered by the bowler.

PITCH: The hard, rectangular surface in the centre of the field between the wickets.

RUN: One point, earned by either running once between the wickets or when a no ball is called. Runs are automatically scored, without the need for running, when the ball reaches or goes over the boundary.

RUN OUT: If a fielding player knocks off the bails with the ball before the batting player reaches the crease, he or she is run out.

SPINNER: A bowler who bowls slow balls that spin as they travel, so they veer to the side. Like a curve ball in baseball.

STRIKE: To be facing the bowler and currently batting is to be "on strike."

STRIKER: The current batter.

STUMPS: The three vertical posts that, along with the bails, make up the wicket.

TEST MATCH: A game with unlimited overs that lasts a full four or five days, only played at the international professional level.

WICKET: The completed set-up of the stumps and the bails. Each out is also called a "wicket." For example, "Shane Warne took three wickets in the last match."

WICKET KEEPER: The fielder who stands close behind the batsman. Akin to the catcher in baseball.

YORKER: A bowling delivery that bounces very close to the batsman's feet. It is very hard to hit or deflect.

ACKNOWLEDGEMENTS

Special thanks go out to my husband, Len, for his cricket expertise, and to the Meraloma Cricket Club for their marvellous dinners. Carrie, Kat, and Amanda were invaluable in shaping this book and making it shine. Thanks are also due to the librarians and booksellers who recognized a need for a cricket book in this series, and to Lorimer for listening to them. Finally, to Brett, Ricky, Shane, Arjuna, Brian, Adam, Sachin, Mark, and Steve, and all the cricketers who inspired my love of the sport, thanks.